Firebow

The town of Firebow lay directly in the path of the marauding Kelly gang as they fled the scene of their latest robbery and killing spree. And for Sheriff Maloney this spelled big trouble, big enough for him to clear the town and reduce it to a ghost of itself.

But when the Kelly mob finally rode in there were more than ghosts to haunt them. Their brutal past had caught up with them in the shape of the mysterious Marshal Carew.

He was no ghost and he was right there – waiting and watching from the shadows.

Firebow

DAN CLAYMAKER

A Black Horse Western

ROBERT HALE · LONDON

ISBN-10: 0-7090-7942-7
ISBN-13: 978-0-7090-7942-2

Robert Hale Limited
Clerkenwell House
Clerkenwell Green
London EC1R 0HT

Typeset by Derek Doyle & Associates, Shaw Heath.
Printed and bound in Great Britain by
Antony Rowe Limited, Wiltshire.

This one for C and B with fondest regard

CHAPTER ONE

He was three score years and ten, and then some, when he finally reached what remained of Firebow.

He had travelled long and hard for more than twelve months, from the sweeping territories of the East and on across the prairies, through blue-grass country to the scrub and brush of the arid deserts, wind-chafed plains, pine forest and mountains.

He had supped with miners, farmers, home-steaders, gold-panners and drifters; drunk with rogues, scumbags, gunslingers and lawmen in a dozen townships; kept the company of cheap women, stood witness at a wedding, dug graves with the grieving for those consigned to Boot Hill, and reckoned no man his better and few, even now, his equal. He was a man with only one purpose, one ambition: to reach Firebow before he breathed his last.

And on that day, in the fading light of late afternoon, with the sun setting deep and the wind whipping the dust and dirt in the deserted street, he came alone and in silence to his destination.

The town was much as he imagined he might find it: empty, broken, rotting at the core, a ghost of its beginnings and promise. It had no heart and its blood had long since dried in the cruel dirt. But some of the structure still stood in defiant reflection of what it had been.

The mercantile, though no longer stocked, had lost its windows but somehow preserved its door from the termite-eaten boardwalk where the few remaining planks lay like the splinters of a ribcage. The barber's shop had lost its roof and a deal of one side, but still carried its sign and displayed a price list as if to tempt, or maybe mock, the lingering ghosts.

The saddlery was no more, save for a counter and a broken chair; the gunsmith's a dark place where anything might lurk if it had a mind to hide, and the sheriff's office had lost most of its rear to the searing winter winds and unforgiving snows.

Only Casey's Palace, the once renowned and expensively furbished saloon and hotel, had somehow defied the elements and creeping ague of time and held its shape if not its glory, even down to the batwings which, on this day, creaked open to the man's careful touch.

He stepped quietly into the sprawling bar, blinked and squinted his tired eyes on the gloom and shadows that looked as if they were in permanent residence, and gazed round him.

The place was draped in cobwebs, hanging like veils, shifting here and there to a draught, the breath of the wind. Dust lay in smears of varying thicknesses, some so deep the man could have buried his fingers in the powdery mass, others scattered and sculpted to drifts of grey deserts across broken tables and chairs, the floor, ledges and shelves and what was left of the bar.

A mirror had yellowed and cracked; bottles and glasses stood incongruously in waiting; a glass cloth had been eaten to shreds. He could make out the remains of a stairway to what had once been the Palace's thriving hotel business, and almost in the empty silence broken only by the moan of the wind, hear the voices of guests, the bar girls and their anxious customers.

He stiffened, sniffed, placed the tips of his fingers on a table at his side, and swallowed on a dry, dusty throat. Damn it, he thought, the place was as near alive as made no odds, but not with those still breathing. He was in the company of ghosts; faces watching him, bodies drifting by him. The ghosts of yesterday.

And then he heard the creak at his back and the scuff of a very living footfall.

CHAPTER TWO

He turned slowly, making no attempt to ease aside the folds of his coat covering a holstered Colt. His eyes narrowed as he squinted to make out the shape of the man silhouetted at the batwings in the glow of late afternoon light.

A young man, tall, straight, confident. He carried a Winchester, levelled and aimed, but he would not be for firing on a whim. He would weigh his odds, figure his chances, and keep that gaze steady and concentrated.

'Howdy,' said the man, the merest flicker of a smile at his lips.

The Winchester prodded instinctively into space. The young fellow grunted, but stood his ground without the shift of a limb. 'Howdy,' he murmured, a touch reluctantly.

The man took a half step.

'Easy,' came the warning, the rifle levelling again. 'Stay right where you are.'

The man shrugged. 'Town ain't exactly teemin' with places to be, is it?' he grinned.

'Who are you? What you doin' here?'

'Might ask the same of yourself. Wouldn't have taken you for bein' resident.'

'I ain't,' said the young man, his gaze shifting quickly as if to establish that the man was alone. 'Got a place to the north. Coupla miles up the trail. I was born here. Visit from time to time. Old memories. What's your reason?'

'Oh, it's a long story.' The man winced. 'You mind if I find some place to sit down, young fella? These old bones of mine don't stay the pace like they once did.'

The Winchester shifted to indicate one of the few standing tables and chairs. 'And you keep your hands where I can see 'em,' said the young man, moving closer through the shaft of light from the 'wings. 'So how come you fetch up in this dead hole?' he added, his curiosity narrowing his gaze, his grip still tense on the rifle.

'Like I say, a long story.' The man showed his hands palms down on the dusty table as he took his seat wearily. 'Yeah, long story, long ride.' He sighed. 'Know somethin', young fella, I been a whole year and some gettin' here? Quite a distance.'

'A year?' frowned the fellow, for the first time easing his fingers on the Winchester. 'Hell, wouldn't have reckoned anybody right-minded figurin' for Firebow bein' worth a year of his life. Place is dead, mister. Been dead for years. I'd reckon for even the ghosts bein' past it.'

The man grunted. 'Name's Chace, Walter Chace,' he said quietly.

11

The young man shifted, nodded, uncertain for a moment of how, or if, to respond. 'Carr,' he said at last. 'Caleb Carr. Pleased to meet you.' The rifle fell a fraction.

'Sam Carr's son? That who you are?'

'S'right. Sam Carr was my Pa. Been dead these past five years.' The young fellow swallowed. 'Did you know him?'

Chace grunted again and slid his hands slowly towards the edge of the table. 'Look, I ain't here for trouble-makin' – too long in the tooth for that – and I sure as hell ain't lookin' to harm no one, so why don't you ease up on that rifle there and find another chair.'

'How come you knew my Pa?' Carr persisted, the rifle stiffening again. 'He never mentioned nobody by the name of Chace.'

'Well, I guess he wouldn't, seein' as how he didn't know me. I happened along of his name when I heard tell of how it was Firebow fell to its miserable fate.'

The young man stepped closer, the Winchester bristling. 'That was a long time ago and most of what you hear told ain't fact,' he snapped. 'There's a whole heap of stories handed out, accounts that don't bear nothin' to the truth of it – and most mouthed by men who ain't never so much as set a foot in this town, let alone stood witness to the events.'

Carr's anger welled in a sudden beading of sweat on his brow, a glint in his eyes that burned through the shafted glare of the light. He stared hard and without blinking.

Chace lifted his hands in a gesture of submission. 'Easy there, young fella, easy,' he soothed. 'I ain't sayin' as how I *believed* all I heard. No, I ain't sayin' that. In fact, I got to thinkin' – real thinkin', mark you – that there's mebbe a deal more to the stories of Firebow than meets the eye.'

'You bet there is!' echoed Carr. 'There's the truth, and that's what ain't told, not never.'

'Precisely,' smiled Chace. 'That's it in one: the truth. And it's because of that, young fella, that I turned the nose of that old nag of mine to the trail for Firebow and just kept on ridin'.'

Carr frowned and swallowed. 'Mister, that don't make no sense by my reckonin'.'

' 'Course it does,' beamed Chace, raising his arms, his smile widening. 'Heck, see it from where I'm sittin'. There I was, rottin' out my closin' years in them two-bit Eastern towns, driftin' from one to the other, almost waitin' on death, listenin' to all the stories about big guns, big men, grown bigger with the tellin' of their so-called exploits; hearin' more often than I cared to count about how Firebow had died, the men who had aided that death, the hundred and one reasons for it; the decent, the downright bad and the all-time gruesome sonsofbitches involved. . . . The hell, I thought, what's the real story of Firebow, the true hand-on-heart account of what happened out there? I resolved to go find out. Why not? I have no home to speak of, no kin, I ain't never been wed, the years are few and thinnin' fast. But I sure as hell got one almighty curiosity. Comes with age! So here I am. I made it, and darn me if I didn't get real lucky in runnin' across no less than Sam Carr's son straight off. How about that?'

Caleb Carr was silent for a long minute. His stare dimmed, the grip on the Winchester eased, the light at his back softened in the late afternoon sun. Shadows began to creep and thicken. The man facing him did not move, not so much as a finger. He simply watched through damp, tired eyes set like soft pools in the creased and weathered features of his face, and waited.

'You want to hear the real story of Firebow like it truly was?' said the young man at last.

'That's right,' murmured Chace. 'Just as it really happened.'

'I was a mite too young to see it all, but what I didn't witness with my own eyes, Pa filled in a hundred times in his tellin' and recollectin' of them days.'

Chace's smile flickered briefly. 'Then if I'm to hear an account as authenticated by Sam Carr and told by his son, I shall die a contented man. So ease aside that piece, young fella, pull up a chair, and begin. . . .'

CHAPTER THREE

There had been a high sun through days of thick, balmy heat for most of that summer as it deepened over the already arid dirt lands surrounding Firebow. Dead brush and scrub dried to tinder, creek streams lay parched and barren under the merciless blaze, rock shade offered scant relief, and the nights were almost as unyielding as the days.

Tempers could fray and snap in an instant in such conditions. Folk got picky and listless. Some men sought day-long solace at the bar of the Palace where proprietor Myram Casey welcomed the boost in sales with a permanently fixed smile and an open house on credit. Others simply languished and lazed their days away with as little effort as possible.

Doc Parker found himself extra busy with bouts of stomach disorders, heat fevers, exhaustion, dehydration, and hangovers. No man, woman or child seemed free of disorders of one kind or another and Doc, along with his patients, could only hope and pray that the rains came early that year on the first cooler winds from the north.

But for Sheriff Jim Maloney, the north had been uppermost in his thoughts since the now long forgotten spring.

There had been reports reaching him through travellers, drifters and wagon bosses who occasionally reined up short of Firebow for supplies, that the bank at the northern town of Murchison had been hit – 'cleaned out, so I hear,' one had reported – by the notorious Kelly gang.

News of a bank raid anywhere was bad news at any time. News of Elmore Kelly and his bunch of gunslingers, rapists and robbers being within a hundred miles of a town was enough to alert and set on edge the nerves of the toughest of lawmen.

And Jim Maloney was no slouch when it came to upholding the law.

First account of any substance of the heist had come with a lone traveller who had cleared Murchison a month back. 'Raid's the talk of the territory back there,' he had told Maloney in the quiet of the sheriff's office. 'On everybody's lips, and in a dozen versions. Facts is facts, though: five men dead, includin' the marshal, one woman, and a handful wounded. And Murchison's fifty, sixty, seventy – who knows – thousands of dollars the poorer. Tell you somethin', Mr Maloney, a raid like that is enough to bankrupt a whole territory, and probably will.' The traveller had cleared the sweat from his face before adding darkly, 'And not a scratch on them Kelly varmints.'

Maloney had urged the traveller not to say too

16

much around Firebow until, as he put it, 'we've got a clearer picture'. But he was whistling on the wind. The Kelly gang's exploits and reputation had always been the very meat and bone of news, gossip, rumour-mongering and fast-growing legend. Where Elmore Kelly led his gang was where the world began and ended for many.

Even so, most folk reasoned, Murchison was a long, long ways away. Events there, however devastating, were hardly likely to ricochet as far south as Firebow. Or, as one old, pipe-smoking, whiskey-supping resident had put it, 'When you've got that much money frettin' like a bad burr in your pants, Firebow don't figure none in your reckonin' of how to spend it!'

But the stories and second-hand accounts had persisted and circulated fast through the town.

'I heard say as how fifteen were gunned down,' a drifter had announced to a crowded Palace bar. 'No mercy. Men, women, even babes. Anybody just about anywhere who happened to cross the path of the Kellys.'

Another, liberally plied with whiskey, had declared, 'Main Street at Murchison was red with blood; runnin' with it. And the stench of death was thick as grease. Thicker. They do claim, and I ain't doubtin' it, that there's ghosts abroad even now. Moanin' folk, drippin' with their own blood. . . .'

The amount actually taken from the bank quickly rose to $100,000 and beyond. 'Wouldn't surprise me to hear as how a quarter-million's linin' the Kelly boys' pockets,' a wagon boss had pondered between helping to hump sacks of flour to a waiting buckboard and blowing smoke from a fat cigar. 'Sooner my outfits cross the Rockies, the better. Can't come soon enough. And for why? Because I ain't for figurin' on the Kellys bein' of a home-makin', pioneerin' nature. Nossir!'

It had taken some weeks – and a shortage of travelling folk passing through – for talk of the raid and the Kelly gang to subside.

Doc Parker pondered the matter along with livery owner, Sam Carr, and Sheriff Maloney over a cool late night beer on the back veranda of his clapboard home. 'Well, I for one ain't sorry to hear the last of the tale for the time bein'. Heck, we got enough to cope with here in this heat. As far as I'm concerned the Kellys can keep right on ridin' to wherever it is they're headin'. . . .'

And they, could he have only known, were words that would come to haunt him.

Another two weeks were to pass before news of the Kelly gang surfaced again. And it came with the shock of a gunshot.

The lone rider had reached Firebow shortly after noon on a day that had seemed to many to be hotter than any before it. The stranger watered his mount, hitched it in the deepest shade he could find, dusted himself down and made for the Palace with only one thought in mind.

Two cold beers later, he had relaxed, mopped the last of the grime and sweat from his face and settled at the bar to appreciate a third beer taken at a slower rate. It was then, with the twenty or so regular afternoon customers at their usual tables, that the stranger announced he had just travelled through from the swing station at Russell Creek some forty miles or so to the west.

'The station as was, I should say,' he had continued to an increasingly attentive audience. 'T'ain't a station no more, and won't be again by my reckonin'. It's gutted. Burned out. Gone. Finished. Just a pile of charred timber and ashes.'

'There's been a fire out there?' said a red-faced man.

'I'll say – and some!' The stranger had quipped. 'Place had been torched; set alight as deliberate as spittin'. And talk is as how it was the doin' of the Kelly gang.'

It was mention of the Kellys that jolted the bar and its customers to sudden concentration and sent one man hurrying to rouse Sheriff Maloney.

The stranger, sensing a captive audience had told his story in an earthy, matter-of-fact tone with few trimmings and no apparent side to an opinion.

'Drifted into Russell out of Bayonet, makin' my way east to the rivers. Plan on doin' some trappin' and huntin' out Cooney Pines way. Anyhow, that's as mebbe. Point is I made for Russell figurin' on restin' up there a day or so before pushin' on to Firebow. That was about the fondest hope I ever did hold!

'No doubtin' as to what had happened. Plain as a man's nose. Station had been ransacked, pillaged, looted and wrecked – call it what you will

19

– and by one helluva determined bunch. Whole sight more than one man obviously; a handful, mebbe more. Anyhow, there was little left that might be salvaged. Not a stick of furniture, not a pot or pan; not so much as a stitch of blanket that would cover a fella. I tell you, that was some sight. A hell-hole of destruction. And then the sonsofbitches had gone and torched it, would you believe? Senseless. Madness.'

The stranger had gulped gratefully at his beer and had it refilled instantly by an eager barman.

'But what about Charlie Lamb?' a man at a table had piped, to murmurs of agreement. 'Charlie's been runnin' that station since the stage route opened. Charlie *is* Russell Creek. Always has been. So what happened to him?'

'Well, he ain't the station manager no more, that's for certain,' said the stranger, wiping the rime of froth from his lips. 'Nossir. Charlie Lamb is dead. Dead and buried right there at Russell Creek.'

The customers, the barman, the few bar girls, even the scavenging dog lurking at the 'wings had fallen into a stunned silence where nothing moved and not a sound drifted across the shimmering heat-haze.

'Them scumbags who did the torchin' killed Charlie?' eased a soft, fearful voice across the bar.

'You bet. As I understand it from the account told to me by Charlie's nearest neighbours – that's the Carson family out on the homesteadin' spread nearby – it was a couple of days before the routine stage pulled in, found the devastation and the body of Charlie Lamb. He'd been shot in the back and just left where he lay. Stage folk did their best to bury him decent back of what remained of the station. Whole affair was reported down the line as far west as Drover's Town. Talk is there's a marshal pickin' up the trail.'

'But how can they be certain it was the Kelly gang?' asked a bulky-gutted man at the 'wings.

'Oh, they're certain. Very certain,' said the stranger, before taking another gulp of his beer. 'Elmore Kelly left a scrawled message on a strip of bedsheet nailed to one of the few standin' timbers.'

'What did it say?' croaked an old-timer, peering through a cloud of pipe smoke.

'Simple enough. There was no messin'. It said: "The Kelly Gang Rides On". It had been written in Charlie Lamb's blood.'

CHAPTER FOUR

The stranger rode out of Firebow at first light the following day, anxious, as he put it, to clear the territory before the Kelly boys bit any deeper into it.

'Darn me if he ain't the only one thinkin' similar,' a townsman had groaned at the stranger's departure. 'Russell ain't that far away. Trail's easy and open. Hell, there ain't nothin' to say the Kellys ain't headin' straight for Firebow.'

But why should they, another had asked? What earthly use was a place like Firebow to a bunch of loud-mouthed, fast-shooting sonsofbitches who had just pulled off the territory's biggest bank raid and were looking for somewhere to spend their ill-gotten gains?

If that in fact was what they intended.

It was Doc Parker who raised the doubt. 'Goin' about clearin' the trail in a mighty peculiar way if that's their figurin',' he reasoned. 'Why stop at Russell? Why not take what they needed at some remote homestead? Why choose a regularly used and known swing station on the main trail? Why kill Charlie, loot and torch the place? And why, in the name of sanity, leave a message sayin' as how you did it?'

'Vanity,' had been Myram Casey's conclusion. 'Just that. An absolute, one hundred per cent conviction that they're untouchable, beyond the reach of any law or lawman. That raid's gone to their heads. Now they figure they can do anythin' anywhere they choose. And they're goin' to show it whenever they get the chance. I seen it in men before.'

'Mebbe they were hooched-up,' Sam Carr had mused. 'Mebbe they were out of their heads – drunk on a whole sight more than liquor. I seen that in men too.'

'Well, whatever, they'll mebbe just keep ridin', as fast and far as they like,' Casey had added, seeking out a cigar from an elaborately tooled leather case and lighting it. 'Somebody will catch up with 'em one day.'

'Mebbe that somebody is already catching up,' Doc had offered quietly.

Sam had shifted uncomfortably and frowned. 'What you sayin', Doc?'

'Just considerin'. Look at it another way: leavin' that scrawled message at Russell could have been intended for somebody *they already knew* was on their trail and followin'. Somebody they expected to reach Russell soon after the stage. Somebody, let's say, like a lawman. Somebody, gentlemen, they *want* to follow them.'

*

23

Doc's figuring had spread through the town like blown dust, its implications not requiring too keen a mind to fathom through.

'Damn it, if that's the case, it means the Kellys will stay with the main trail, baitin' whoever's followin' all down the line,' a bushy bearded fellow had reckoned, taking his place at the Palace bar. 'And that leads—'

'You don't have to spell it out,' Casey had urged, from among a clutch of his bar girls. 'Trail leads directly here. Forty miles at best. Three days' ridin'. Four in this heat.'

'Hell,' a man had gasped, breaking into a colder sweat.

'But if Sheriff Maloney ain't so sure,' Casey had continued hurriedly. 'Leastways, he wasn't a couple of hours back. . . .'

Now Maloney was in two minds. Doc's theorizing had some merit – maybe a whole sight more than could be fathomed right now – but there were other, more immediate considerations. 'For example, water, fresh mounts – the gang ain't goin' nowhere without any one of them, 'specially the water in these conditions. Take it from me there ain't a creek bed out there that ain't scorched bone dry. So where are they gettin' this water, if not for themselves, then a priority for their horses?'

A day later he was to have the grim answer.

The Taylor family rolled their trail-worn wagon into town in the last of the day's light. Sam Carr had been at the livery noting their slow progress for close on a half-hour and was the first to greet the travellers.

'Howdy,' he had smiled, stepping closer as the driver heaved the team to a halt. 'Just made it. Another twenty minutes and it'd have been full dark. Night falls awful fast these parts. You want I should look to the horses?'

'A whole sight more than the horses, mister,' the driver had croaked, jumping down to the ground, his eyes tired and staring. 'I got my wife and young 'un back here. Wife's in a bad way, and the kid ain't much better.' He ran a shaky hand over the unblinking gaze as if to wipe away some memory. 'They need a doctor, fast.'

'Sure, sure, we got a doc,' Sam had soothed. 'One of the best. I'll go get him. Your woman got the fever?'

'No fever, mister. We were attacked twenty miles or so back. Us and our good friends the Smithsons. They didn't make it. We got lucky.'

'Bushwhackers?'

'The Kelly gang.'

'Hell,' Sam had gulped. 'Then I'd best get the sheriff along of Doc Parker.'

Seated in Maloney's office an hour later, a mug of hot coffee to hand, his wife and daughter in the watchful care of Doc, Ned Taylor had told his story with brutal frankness.

'Came at us like thunder, six of 'em. Seemed like more. We were travellin' just ahead of the Smithsons when they struck. Sun up. We'd been movin' no more than an hour. Came across the dirt plain like wild things. Whoopin', yellin', cursin'. Might've been liquored up, but that was no booze drivin' them animals on. That was madness.

'They seemed to eye up the two outfits, then cut the Smithsons apart. Turned them off the trail and brought them to a halt a quarter-mile or so behind us. I reined up, swung my team round all set to beat the hell back there, do what I could for our good friends. But Myra, my wife, urged caution. Hell, we were not for fightin', never have been. Don't hold with shooters save to hunt. But this. . . .

'Anyhow, I waited, just watchin' as them scum dragged Mrs Smithson from the wagon and tore the clothes from her like they were frenzied wolves. Two of 'em set about lootin' the outfit, throwin' aside everythin' save food, the water barrel, canteens, provisions. That's all they were interested in. Food, water, Mrs Smithson.'

The man had paused a moment, his gaze settling on the soft streams of steam lifting from the coffee. He might have been staring through a mist to the vagueness of images past.

'They shot Jim Smithson through the head, right there in front of his wife, then went back to rapin' her 'til she too lay lifeless. I tell you, mister. . . .'

Taylor's voice had trailed away before he resumed, his tone lower, near exhausted. 'It was then that one of 'em, a younger, blazin'-eyed fella, turned his attention on us. Came at us in a whirlwind. We got back to the trail, my wife along of me up top, the daughter, Jessie, back of the wagon. But that sonofabitch, soon drew level, fired a shot clean through Myra's shoulder. I tell you straight up, I thought we were starin' death in the face. But for some reason – I ain't sure what – the fella chasin' us got called back by the others. I can see his face now, sweat-soaked, smilin', eyes like fires. Yelled out as how the Kelly gang never forgot and he'd be back to take the women.

'And that was it, he was gone. We raced on, blind, just hittin' the trail fast as we could, not carin' a damn where we were, or headin', just so long as we were clear of them scumbags. Nothin' we could do for the Smithsons. They were dead and their wagon looted. Last we saw was the smoke as the Kellys torched the whole shebang, outfit, bodies and all, I dare say. The Smithsons had been our friends best part of our lives.

'Seein' this town and Mr Carr here waitin' on us, was like a prayer bein' answered, Sheriff. And that's for a fact. A prayer answered. . . .'

CHAPTER FIVE

'All the prayin' in Creation ain't goin' to change what we're facin'. He'd be a fool as said other.' The townsman replaced his beer glass, wiped his mouth with the back of his hand, then lit a cheroot to add to the thickening haze of smoke in the Palace saloon. 'Them Taylor folk got lucky. Real lucky. Doc says as how the woman will recover and the daughter will come out of her shock given time. But, hell, when you get to think of what might have happened. . . .'

'What are we goin' to do, that's what I want to hear,' moaned a short, skinny fellow sporting an oversize derby. 'Them rats are twenty miles back, accordin' to the wagon folk. Twenty miles – that ain't no distance. Why, the Kellys could be here come noon t'morrow. Sooner if they've a mind.'

A man at a table drummed his fingers rhythmically. 'They'll be of a mind, make no mistake. Water, somewhere to rest up, that's what they'll have a mind for; that and free women.' He glanced quickly at the bar girls hovering around Casey. 'Best keep them gals out of sight, Myram.'

The proprietor adjusted his glowing cigar clamped between his teeth. 'Ain't nobody – and that includes the Kelly boys – lays a finger on my girls without my say-so. Rules is rules. I've built my business reputation on rules, and I ain't for changin' now.'

'Yeah, well, I can hear the Kelly gang's answer to that; fast lead in the gut before you can blink,' quipped a man at the batwings as he stared into the deserted, night-black street where only a handful of lanterns glimmered softly. 'So what are we goin' to do?' he added coldly. 'Sit around talkin' and drinkin'? Ride out there and get to the Kellys before they get to us? Anybody got the stomach for that? Or are we goin' to set some store by Doc's reckonin' and wait on whoever might be trackin' the gang to catch up? That's mebbe the longest shot, but he could be right. Fact is, whatever we do don't change the Kellys closeness one snitch. They're at the back door.'

'I say we go out and fight,' said a tall youth, hooking his thumbs in his belt. 'Meet 'em face on. Shoot it out. Stop the rats right there in their tracks.'

'Just like that,' mused an old-timer. 'Kill off half the town in the doin'. No, I don't think so.'

'So what are you for?' clipped a man at his back. 'Sittin' it out and bein' shot in your bed?'

'Maybe the Kellys will ride some place else?' piped a bar girl through a flush of blushing.

'Nice thought, my dear,' smiled Casey, patting the girl's shoulder, 'but unlikely. At twenty miles

29

away, they're too close to miss us. No, they'll be here, sure enough.'

'You're right, Myram,' agreed the bushy-bearded fellow, draining the dregs of a whiskey bottle to his waiting glass. 'They'll be here, large as life and twice as violent. Won't be long before they've taken over. Won't be nothin' they won't take: food, whiskey, horses, stores, provisions, then the women and girls, one by one 'til there ain't nothin' that ain't been touched and fouled by them scumbags. That's the Kelly gang, you can bet to it. And when they're done, we'll bury the dead, comfort the broken, scrape t'gether whatever's left and try livin' with the ghosts of it all.' He finished his drink with a flourish and banged the glass back to the table. 'That's what we're facin', don't doubt it.'

'But not if we ain't here,' came a voice from the boardwalk as the 'wings creaked open and Sheriff Maloney strode into the bar.

'Ain't here?' croaked the man in the derby standing to his full height. 'You mean . . . you mean— Hell, what do you mean, Sheriff?'

Maloney made his way to the bar, turned and faced the gathering. 'Pullin' out. Leavin'. Every man, woman, child, horse and hound. Clearin' the town 'til there ain't nothin' left save the timbers, the glass, some stores and liquor, odd bits and pieces of provisions – but no folk, not so much as a breath of one. I'm proposin' we desert this town and leave the Kelly gang with only the ghosts of it.'

The town men stared. The bar girls gazed open-mouthed. Cigar smoke curled and drifted as if lost. Glasses, half raised to lips, remained suspended. Myram Casey swallowed and blinked.

'Am I hearin' you right there, Sheriff?' gulped the proprietor. 'Are you seriously suggestin' we leave Firebow to the Kellys; that we just pack our bags and leave; throw up our businesses, our homes, our lives, damnit, and trail out to. . . ? To where precisely? You thought of that?'

The townsmen murmured among themselves. A raised voice piped, 'Crazy!' The bar girls chattered like birds. Casey gripped the lapels of his embroidered coat and glared. Maloney poured himself a measure of whiskey from a waiting bottle on the bar and sank it quickly. 'I've been talkin' it over just now with Doc Parker and Sam Carr and we're all agreed, if we stay here and fight it out with Kelly and his boys there's goin' to be an awful lot of blood spilled and innocent lives lost, not to mention property looted and ransacked. The loss of goods and property we can live with – folk can build again and replenish stocks – but you can't go messin' with human lives, not when there's a chance they can be saved, 'specially the young.'

'Can't argue with that,' said the old-timer, scratching his stubble.

'Nobody is,' snapped Casey, 'but there's a helluva difference between that and turnin' your back on a business that's taken a lifetime to build.'

'And five seconds to lose if you get the wrong side of Kelly lead,' returned the old man.

Maloney raised a hand for quiet. 'Doc and Sam

and me figure we could load all the wagons we can lay a hand to with as much as we'll need and pull out to Bottom Creek. Nobody goes that way much – there ain't nothin' there – and we could hole up safe for as long as it takes.'

'And how long's that goin' to be?' clipped the youth.

'Two weeks. A month at best. We don't reckon for the Kelly boys stayin' long in a ghost town.'

The bushy-bearded man came to his feet and stepped to Maloney's side. 'There's a deal of sense in what the sheriff's sayin' here. And I for one figure it might just work – if we get real organized and work together fast.'

'Mebbe,' called the man at the 'wings, 'but we're goin' to need to know what the Kellys are doin'. Somebody's got to keep a watch on things here.'

'Sam and me are volunteerin' for that,' said Maloney. 'Town's safety is my responsibility anyhow, and Sam figures that bein' one of the first settlers here, and him being alone now since his wife died and there's his son, Caleb, to build a future for, he's got a close interest in what tran-spires. Doc says he's the obvious choice to look to folk at the creek, and Seb Sloan across there at the mercantile is goin' to handle the food and beddin' side of things. He's checkin' out stocks right now.

'We need the rest of you to get to helpin' and plannin' where you can and work at it through the night. I'm reckonin' on Kelly and his scumbags bein' here soon after noon tomorrow. That don't give us long, so every hour is vital, but it can be

32

done. Damn it, it's got to be done for all our sakes. What do you say?'

But it was going to be another long twenty minutes before Maloney had raised a consensus to reduce Firebow to a ghost town. Sam, Doc and Seb Sloan had finally joined him to support the proposal.

'I ain't one for backin' off from a challenge, and I sure ain't no coward, but, hell, to wait on the Kellys wreckin' this town in a bloodbath ain't no way at all,' Doc had argued. 'We can make it to Bottom Creek, sure we can, make it and survive.'

'You bet,' Sam had offered in support. 'I can raise most of the horses needed, fair few wagons along of 'em; there's feed and water to reckon to, but, damnit, we can cope.'

'And there ain't no problem with supplies; I've got a storeful,' the storekeeper promised. 'Enough to keep us goin' for at least a month. Sheriff says I should leave behind sufficient to keep the Kelly gang from goin' in search of food. Same goes for you, Myram. Leave just enough liquor to keep the rats happy. All the cheap stuff.'

'I would have you know that the Palace ain't never sold—' But Casey's protest had been drowned by the gathering's raised voices and scraping of chairs as they came to agreement and prepared to set about the task facing them.

'T'ain't goin' to be easy,' a man, rolling up his sleeves, had murmured to Doc.

'Survival never has,' smiled Doc. 'Ask the Taylor family. But they've made it – this far.'

CHAPTER SIX

It was 10.30 by Doc's pocket timepiece on an already hot, cloudless morning when Sam Carr and Seb Sloan announced that the line of wagons was ready to roll.

'Loaded to the canvas and not a thing carted as ain't needed,' said Sam, patting the side of the lead wagon to be driven by bushy beard.

'S'right, Sheriff,' grinned the man. 'Got enough of everythin' here as a fella needs to survive.'

'Food supplies for a month,' confirmed Sloan. 'All the water we can carry. Folk have packed only clothes and personal possessions. We ain't leavin' a deal for the Kellys.'

'Keep the line close and steady once you're clear of town,' said Maloney. 'I reckon for you havin' a two-hour start. You'll make the creek by nightfall. But remember, no stoppin' unless you're absolutely forced, and nobody's to come back here, not for nothin'. Either Sam or me will get news to you of what's happenin'. Doc's in charge once you get settled. And good luck to you – all of you.'

'Hell, Mr Maloney, it's you and Sam as will be needin' all the luck goin',' said the bushy-bearded man climbing aboard his outfit. 'Just don't get tanglin' with them varmints. They ain't worth it.' He raised an arm, waved it as a signal to the others and cracked the reins for the team to take the strain and get underway.

Sam and the sheriff watched in silence as the line passed along the street heading out to the main trail. A slow drift of dust shimmered in the heat. Wheels and timbers creaked and moaned under the weight of their burdens; few voices were heard and no one called out. Some nodded as they caught the sheriff's eye, some murmured encouragement among their farewells. Some of the women dabbed at tears, others comforted bemused youngsters.

The old-timer puffed at a corncob pipe and raised his hat. Casey still sniffed his reluctance and stared forlornly at the Palace as it faded from view in the cloud of dust. The bar girls, seated together in one wagon, clung to their valises containing clothes and perfumes, and looked round them bewildered and suddenly vulnerable. The line moved on. The dust thickened. The creaks grew thinner and softer.

Doc Parker brought up the rear mounted on his familiar roan mare, his medical bag strapped tight to his saddle. 'Worst part of this is leavin' you two behind,' he said, reining the mare to a halt. 'And I ain't sure even now as it's the right thing to be doin'. But – like you say, somebody's got to know what's happenin'. The Taylors are stayin' with us. Very wise under the circumstances.' He watched the trundling wagons for a moment, 'Goddamnit if this ain't one helluva mess, but you just get us when you need help.'

Maloney thanked him, patted the mare and urged Doc on. 'You've got the biggest job of all keepin' the town alive and well. Get to it!'

It was another hour before the wagons had finally cleared town and disappeared in the dust haze towards Bottom Creek.

Maloney grunted and narrowed his gaze against the glare as he scanned the deserted street. 'Just hope we're doin' the right thing here, Sam,' he said, clearing a glaze of sweat from his face.

'Too late now,' returned Sam, tightening his grip on his Winchester. 'It's done, and for the best by my figurin'. If we save lives, that's the whole top and bottom of it.' He watched Maloney for a moment before adding, 'Time we made ourselves scarce. Let's go find ourselves a lair.'

Soon their shadows were lost and the street lay silent and empty.

It was the touch of Maloney's hand on Sam's arm that stirred the livery owner from his dozing sleep in the long abandoned storeroom above the saddlery.

Sam blinked, wiped the dust from his mouth and trained his still clearing gaze on the sheriff's nod to the smeared, cobwebbed window. 'Company,' murmured Maloney, indicating the swirl of a dust cloud beyond the far reaches of the street.

Sam eased closer, rubbed the tips of his fingers across the pane, and squinted. 'About a mile out. Ridin' fast.' He swallowed. 'The Kellys?'

'I'd reckon,' said Maloney. 'You figure how many?'

'Six. Mebbe eight.'

The sheriff mopped a spotted bandanna round his neck. 'They're goin' to be a mite thirsty time they hit town. Just hope Casey left enough liquor to keep 'em happy. Don't want the rats tearin' the town apart.'

'They'll get to that soon enough.'

The two men settled to watch and wait, their gazes fixed and tight on the dust cloud, the sweat beading like rain on their brows and faces as the stifling heat of the day grew ever thicker and heavy in the storeroom.

'Charlie Lamb ... the Smithsons ... the Murchison raid, and God knows how many dead before and since. . . . Hell, them Kellys and their sidekicks don't deserve to stay breathin'.' Sam blinked and gulped carefully at a canteen of tepid water. 'You still settin' any store by that talk of a marshal trailin' them?'

'It's leavin' the message that don't make sense. Why, unless you were expectin' it to be read? Why announce so bluntly who you are to the Taylors knowin' full well they're goin' to tell? It's my bettin' the Kellys are wantin' this somebody followin' to keep right on comin'. They know him.

But mebbe more to the point, he knows them. And that could be important.'

Sam grunted and scrubbed at the pane again. 'Gettin' closer. Another couple of minutes and we'll be seein' 'em proper. Ain't that some prospect!'

They rode in, a dozen strong, as grey as ghosts and grim as death. They were tired, hungry and, above all, thirsty. They were mounted on lathered, near exhausted horses, and trailed two heavily laden packs. Firebow, whatever it had to offer, was already a haven.

The dust was still swirling as they dismounted and led their mounts to the water-troughs. Elmore Kelly, the tall, dust-coated leader and elder of the gang, was the first to look round him as he drank from his canteen. His gaze was narrowed and piercing, his eyes like lights on the sprawl of the deserted boardwalks, the silent buildings, the street where not so much as a scavenging hound looked on. His inspection paused at the shadowed door and window of the sheriff's office; moved on to the batwings at the Palace and the dark interior beyond them; shifted again to the mercantile, the barber's shop, the one-time saddlery, then, in a sudden flash of anger, darted to the man at his side.

'This place is deserted,' he growled, spitting into the dirt at his feet. 'A ghost town. Since when? When did this happen?'

His partner shrugged dismissively. 'Wouldn't

know. Ain't never clapped eyes on the place before. What's it matter, anyhow? Town's a town wherever you find 'em. It'll do.'

The elder man's gaze was moving again, back to the boardwalks, the batwings and now towards the livery. 'Get the place looked over,' he ordered. 'Every building, every room. Don't miss nothin', you understand?'

'We restin' up here, boss?' called one of the riders from a distance.

'T'ain't much of a place,' croaked another, wiping his mouth. 'Seems like folk have pulled out.'

'Lead me to that bar back there!' quipped a third man before dunking his head in the water trough and surfacing again like a dripping rat.

'There'll be no liquor 'til these horses are looked to and the money stashed safe,' ordered the tall man again. 'So get to it, damn you.'

Sam Carr cleared the hot, sticky sweat from his face and eased back from the window overlooking the street. 'They're settlin',' he murmured, glancing quickly at Maloney at his side. 'They ain't for ridin' on.'

'Never figured they would. They'll stay as long as it suits, or 'til Elmore there reckons for there bein' somethin' that don't suit.'

'So what do we do now?'

The sheriff rubbed his chin. 'Get closer – if we can. We've got to know exactly what Kelly is thinkin' and doin', and we need to know where they're keepin' the money.'

'You ain't thinkin' of tryin' to take it back, are you?' gulped Sam.

'No, but I'd still like to know.' He pulled away from the window and sat with his back to the wall. 'We'll take it in turns to keep watch, then make a move come nightfall.'

'To where?'

'The saloon. We need to be in there for the night. That's where Kelly will hole-up.'

'Easier said than done,' pondered Sam. 'Gettin' in might not be so difficult; it's gettin' out that bothers me.' He gazed out of the window again where now the dust had settled and the shadows lay like dark limbs in the afternoon glare. A gunslinger lounged on the boardwalk fronting the saloon, his fingers working feverishly in the twirling of a drawn Colt.

He looked, thought Sam, to be waiting for the first easy target to cross his path.

CHAPTER SEVEN

The shot rang out with a roar that rose and thinned to a whine then faded across the evening light to an echo. 'What the hell was all that about?' hissed Sam, shuffling back into the deeper shadows at the rear of the old saddlery. He looked anxiously at Sheriff Maloney who gestured for silence and staying low.

Sam peered through the gloom to the sudden flurry of activity across the street in the Palace bar. Faces appeared at windows; shapes moved like silhouettes through the soft glow of lantern light. Seconds passed. A stiff, waiting silence descended. No sounds. Nothing moving.

'Don't move,' urged Maloney, licking at a thin beading of sweat on his lips.

The batwings creaked open. Two gunslingers straddled the boardwalk, Colts drawn, bodies tensed, eyes gleaming.

'Hal?' called one. 'You out there? What's goin' on?'

Silence.

The man called again, glanced at his partner

indicating they should step down to the street. They moved slowly, watchfully, looking from left to right, training their guns on shadows their eyes could not probe.

'Hal? Hey, what the hell's goin' on out here? You fire that shot?'

Sam swallowed, felt his hand sticky on the butt of his drawn Colt. Damnit, who had fired the shot? And why? He watched as Maloney eased a step forward. 'You see anythin'?' he hissed, shuffling to the sheriff's side.

Maloney gestured for silence again and nodded to the open street where now the shadows and oncoming night had met in an eerily half-lit gloom.

The two men stood close together, their guns loose at their sides, stares fixed on the sprawled body at their feet.

'Who the hell's that?' hissed Sam again.

'One of the gang. Can't be no other.'

'But how . . . who?'

Maloney gestured for them to move to the rear door of the saddlery. 'Back to the window,' he whispered. 'Saloon's goin' to be buzzin' once this hits Elmore Kelly. No place for us. We'll try again later when things have cooled some.'

'But who did the shootin'?' blustered Sam, the sweat beading freely on his face.

Maloney stared deep into the gathering night. 'There's another gun in town,' he murmured.

'There's a gun out there. A mangy, stinkin' sonofabitch with some fancy notion he can handle a shooter.' Bonehead Kelly kicked the spittoon at the corner of the bar and spat into the space it left. 'You want I should go slit the fella's throat, Elmore, or mebbe string him up; or we could use him as target practice for an hour or so?' He hawked and spat again. 'What's with this two-bit town, anyhow? How come there ain't no folk here? How come it's closed up?' The gang leader's wild-eyed, scar-faced brother drank noisily from a bottle of whiskey then slammed it back on the bar. 'Well?' he asked, glaring round the assembled gunslingers.

'Easy there, easy,' said his elder brother Chad, glancing hurriedly at the brooding bulk of Elmore. 'Hal was a good man. We're goin' to miss him, but one shootin' ain't cause for losin' our heads. We'll get the rat who shot him. 'Course we will, but not in the middle of the night, not when it's as black as the inside of a boot out there.'

The watching sidekicks shuffled their backsides, drummed impatient fingers on the table-tops, poured more whiskey, lit cheroots and blew more smoke.

'Know somethin',' said a long-legged man, fingering an empty glass, 'that could be Marshal Carew out there. You thought of that? Mebbe he's caught up at last. Mebbe he's out there right now figurin' how to take us out, one by one. Mebbe Hal's just the first.' He pushed the glass aside. 'Mebbe we should pull out first light. Get this place off our backs. Don't seem a deal of use anyhow. What you reckon?'

'I reckon you talk too much,' said Elmore Kelly, coming to his feet and making his way to the batwings. 'But you're right, mebbe that is Carew out there. Mebbe it was him who took out Hal, like he was sayin': "I'm here". So be it. It's what we've been waitin' for.'

'But not here, eh, Brother?' said Bonehead. 'Not in a two-bit ghost town.'

'This place is perfect,' snapped Elmore. 'Couldn't be better.'

The men were silent for a moment, their gazes concentrated on the gang leader as he made his slow, thoughtful way round the bar, the steps measured, deliberate, paced.

'They knew we were comin',' murmured a sweaty-faced man adjusting his hat. 'Whole town knew. That's why they've gone. Left us with just enough to eat and drink. Mebbe they're plannin'—'

'They ain't plannin' nothin',' said Chad, his concentration fixed on cleaning his fingernails with a toothpick. 'They left because they were scared. Didn't want to face up to the Kelly gang. Rightly so, too. Neither would I!'

The men smiled and tittered, poured more drinks, blew new clouds of smoke.

'Took the women, though,' piped a younger man sullenly. 'Sure as damnit did that, didn't they? Knew what they were doin' there, sure enough. You bet.'

'You moanin' there, Bart?' said Chad, lifting his concentration from his fingernails to the youth

44

and then to Elmore's steady circumnavigation of the saloon. 'A woman mean that much to you? Then I'll get you a woman, young fella. Sure I will. You got any particular preference?'

'Now, hang on there, Chad, I was only sayin'—'

'I heard exactly what you were sayin',' said Chad, examining the tip of the toothpick through a half-closed eye. ' 'Fact I heard every last syllable, and I see your point, Bart. And you take it from Elmore here and me as how you'll get your woman just as soon as we've reckoned with the sonofabitch loose gun out there. . . .'

Chad Kelly reached in a flash of fingers for the empty bottle at his side and threw it directly at the head of the young man.

The young man ducked, but too late as it struck his temple to the jeers and taunts of the others.

'So who's for a killin'?' bawled the gang leader coming to a stamping halt. He glared round the faces turned to him. 'Who's goin' to pack a Winchester at first light and go stalk that rat Carew and shoot him? Which one of you, eh?'

The sullen young man had already sprung to his feet to take up Elmore Kelly's challenge when the clatter of a falling crate or barrel somewhere in the deeper recesses of the rear of the bar closed mouths and stilled limbs.

Chad Kelly motioned to Bonehead to move to the left of the locked rear door leading to the storage rooms and outback buildings. The youth slid away to the right.

45

It was Bonehead who finally crept silently to the door, turned the key softly, reached for the knob and swung the door open with a violent flourish, at the same time blazing two fast shots from a levelled Colt into the dark space.

The echoes of the shots faded to a new silence. 'Go take a look, Bonehead,' ordered Elmore.

The man eased forward like a preying lizard, the eyes of the others watching as if transfixed. 'Don't nobody move,' whispered Chad.

'Mebbe it's Carew in there,' murmured one of the men.

'Quiet!' snapped Elmore.

They waited. The silence gathered. The bar clock ticked sonorously.

It was a full two minutes before Bonehead's voice reached from the darkness. 'Ain't nobody here as I can see,' he called. 'But there's sure as hell been somebody. And recent.' He appeared again in the open doorway. 'Must've knocked up against a crate. But he ain't here now. Disappeared. You want me and some of the boys—'

'I don't want nobody to do nothin'!' bellowed Elmore, stamping to the bar to pour himself a drink which he sank in one wincing gulp. 'All I want is we should put Hal's body some place 'til we can get to buryin' him decent. Then I want somebody to go check on the money. Make sure it's secure. Then we wait. We wait and stay awake. And when it's sun-up, we'll go get Carew.' He poured another drink, sank it, grabbed a three-quarters full bottle and seated himself in a darkened corner of the bar.

Chad Kelly grunted quietly to himself and concentrated his gaze on his fingernails and his dexterity with the toothpick. He had seen his brother in this brooding mood before. And always when Marshal Carew came into their lives.

CHAPTER EIGHT

'That was close. Too close. We got lucky.' Sam Carr handed his canteen to Sheriff Maloney and eased back to the dark window overlooking the street. 'All quiet out there for now,' he murmured, squinting into the night, 'but I guess we stay put 'til first light. Right? No more slippin' through the back entrance to Casey's.' He scratched the stubble on his chin and smiled softly to himself. 'Got in, though, didn't we? And if it hadn't been for that darned crate . . .' The smile faded. 'Who do you figure for this Marshal Carew bein'? You crossed him before?'

Maloney stoppered the canteen, wiped a hand across his mouth and joined Sam at the window. 'Been givin' some thought to that and I ain't come up with an answer. Got to know most of the lawmen hereabouts over the years – sometimes only by name – but Carew don't ring no bells, not for as far back as I can recall. Which ain't provin' nothin' really. Mebbe he's from another territory.'

'Mebbe he's been trailin' the Kelly bunch for some whiles.'

48

Maloney grunted. 'Whatever, the rats out there are ready to show him some respect.'

'Could be they fear him,' said Sam, shifting his weight. 'We heard enough to indicate the fella's no pushover – and he's proved that already. Took out that gunslinger calm as you like.' Sam scratched his chin again. 'Is Carew still here? Do we go find him, make some sort of contact? What you reckon?'

The sheriff stared into the silent, empty, moonlit street where even the shadows seemed to be on tenterhooks. 'I'm goin' to take another look at the saloon. I want to know exactly what the Kellys are doin' and when they're doin' it.'

'Now just you hold on there, mister. . . .' But Sam's protest was already lost on the sultry night air as Maloney slid away across the room and through the rear door to the street below.

An hour passed. Sam dozed; woke with a sudden start, dozed again and blinked on the darkness beyond the window where the low lights in the saloon cast an aura of shabby grey.

He had seen no movements, heard no sounds. Only once had a posted look-out wandered through the batwings to the boardwalk to smoke a cheroot. He had not dallied, fearful perhaps of a probing rifle barrel, a steady aim that might be anywhere, in any one of the buildings facing him, any one of the dark alleyways between them.

So where was Carew, wondered Sam? Still in town, or had he killed his man and ridden out to hole up somewhere in one of the hundred creeks and outcrops in the surrounding country? Would he be back at first light, or was he still here? Was he still watching, still waiting? Had he seen anything of Doc and the townsfolk; perhaps picked up their trail, or crossed close to Bottom Creek?

The questions gnawed at Sam like a dull ache. And as if they were not enough, what had happened to Maloney since making his return to Casey's? Where was the sheriff now; what had he seen? Maybe more to the point, what had he heard?

What if he was discovered? Sam swallowed, shifted his position and scanned the street again. It looked the same as it had always been. The same dried dirt, same shadows in the same positions. And if he were to set foot in it, it would feel the same. The street never changed.

'Hold it,' he hissed to himself, pressing his face closer to the windowpane. There was something. Something different. Or somebody.

A shadow moving slowly. Heading towards the saloon. Pausing. Waiting. Moving on. Hell, thought Sam, supposing it was Carew. Was the lawman planning on getting into the saloon? Did he—?

Another movement, this time at the batwings as a newly woken gunslinger came on guard, stepped to the boardwalk, yawned, stretched and hitched his pants before drawing a Colt and spinning it through his fingers.

He looked to the left, to the right, turned and

spun the piece through a final swirl and holstered it with a thud. Only then did he stop mid-step, wait as if about to turn again, shuffle a few inches forward and fall flat on his face with a sickening thud.

The handle of the knife buried between his shoulder blades glinted for a moment like a savage eye.

Sam continued to watch as the batwings crashed open and the boardwalk filled with the Kelly brothers and their sidekicks.

'Get him inside,' ordered Elmore, glaring into the street as if about to devour it.

Two men lifted the body and moved back slowly to the dim glow in the bar. Chad Kelly, his brothers, Bonehead and Elmore remained in the shadows, their eyes probing the night like lights. Sam, licking nervously at the sweat on his top lip, eased the window open a fraction to catch the drift of their voices.

'Carew,' croaked Bonehead. 'Only Carew would use a blade that way.'

'Don't take no fathomin',' said Chad, stepping to the edge of the boardwalk, his eyes narrowing on the deserted street. 'He's here. He's found us, just like we planned he should. Only trouble is, o'course, he's got an edge. We didn't plan on hittin' a ghost town. Now, we're the only targets. There ain't nobody else here – nobody to hold hostage. In a nutshell, Brothers, we're rats in a barrel. Carew can pick us off just as it suits. And, by my reckonin', that's precisely what he'll do.'

'I don't like your tone there, Chad,' said Bonehead. 'Seems to me like you're sayin' as how we're already backs to the wall with this son-ofabitch marshal. That ain't Kelly thinkin'. That ain't how we planned it. T'ain't Kelly reckonin'.'

'Mebbe not,' murmured the elder brother, 'but he's right. We are in a barrel. So where are the townsfolk? Where they hidin'? Damnit, a whole town can't just disappear.'

Chad lit a cheroot, leaving the match to flare and burn to its tip. He dropped the charred strip to the dirt. 'Just so. Where are they? Not far away to my mind.' He turned sharply. 'Let's go figure it, eh?'

The three men pushed open the 'wings and disappeared into the dimly lit gloom of the bar. Sam eased back from the window and pushed his hat to the back of his head. 'Heck,' he muttered, 'if that means what I think it means. . . .' He settled his hat again and tensed as the door to the room creaked to the touch of Maloney's return.

'You see all that?' asked the sheriff, mopping his brow.

'Saw it and heard the talk,' said Sam, 'and I'd wager Kelly's goin' to hunt down the townsfolk. He needs 'em. The rat's lookin' for a shield to get himself behind and draw this Carew fella into the open.'

'I saw him. Not close, but close enough. He's a lawman all right. I can tell.'

'He see you?'

'Mebbe not, and even if he did, he didn't want contact. I'd figure for this fella workin' alone.'

Sam went back to the window. 'They won't show themselves again 'til sun-up. Time for one of us to report to Doc, let the others know what's happenin'. And I'm volunteerin' if you reckon you can hold on here for a while.'

'No problem. Go when you're ready. Sooner the better. If Kelly decides to make a move at first light, we all need to be prepared. But remember, no takin' chances. When you're dealin' with rattlers you walk round them real slow. And you never look away.'

CHAPTER NINE

Sam had left within the hour, slid silently away to the old barn at the back of the mercantile where he and Maloney had hitched their mounts, and gone like a ghost rider to the trail for Bottom Creek.

. Maloney, alone in the dusty, cobwebbed room above the saddlery, had settled to catch whatever fitful sleep he could before first light. But his dozing was troubled by thoughts of how Sam would make out, of where Carew had hidden himself and what he planned from here on, and not least of what was going through the Kelly brothers' minds.

Elmore and Chad would make the final decisions, but Maloney would wager that uppermost in their reckoning would be the need to avoid another loss. One man taken out was bad enough; two was approaching a crisis; any more and they would be within a spit of standing alone.

Carew would be figuring along the same lines. But how long would he wait, wondered Maloney, jerking awake for the third time in what seemed as many minutes?

He came to his feet, crossed to the deeper darkness at the back of the room and stared into the vague blur of light at the smeared window. Give it another half-hour, he reckoned, and he would head once again for the saloon.

He had stayed lucky this far. The Kellys were still unaware of his presence. As far as they were concerned, they had only Carew to worry about. He would keep it that way. Meantime, he thought, crossing to the window again, the shadows were still and empty.

Or so it seemed.

'Myself and Bonehead. That's all it'll take. Give us a few hours come first light and we'll know. That I promise.'

Chad Kelly stared across the table at his brother Elmore and waited for the man to look up from the glass he turned through his fingers. It was a while before he grunted and pushed the glass aside. 'Which way? You ain't got any notion to where them townfolk are holed up. Could be miles out,' he said, his eyes lifting like white moons.

'I've been givin' that some thought,' reflected Chad, easing back in his chair. 'I figure for them bein' a whole sight closer than we reckon. I don't think they'd have had too much warnin' on our headin' this way, and when you get to lookin' close, this town ain't long been abandoned. It's a whole sight too clean. There ain't enough dust. So . . . what if they pulled out only hours before we rode in; they wouldn't have gotten far, not with a line of wagons, old folk and young 'uns to look to. They probably ain't more than a few miles away. Somewhere deserted. A hidden creek some place, that's what I'll be lookin' for.' He reached for the bottle in the centre of the table and poured himself a measure. 'All you and the boys have got to do is keep an eye on Carew – if he shows himself'

'He'll show sooner or later,' said Elmore. 'And make a mistake. You can bet to it. And when he does. . . .'

'Yeah, well, you just save some of that son-ofabitch for Bonehead and me!'

Sheriff Maloney eased away from the chink in the storeroom wall that gave him a view of the Palace bar, and wiped a hand over his face. Hell, he thought, how long would it take for Chad Kelly to discover Bottom Creek? And what then? He just hoped Sam had ridden hard and straight.

He pressed his face back to the wall and peered through the chink. A half-dozen saddle-bags had been piled in the deepest, darkest corner of the bar. The money from the raid in Murchison; the blood-soaked spoils so many had already died for. Maloney swallowed and began to sweat again.

How come all this was happening in his town, among the folk he had lived and worked with for years? How come it had been Firebow's bad luck to draw the misery of the Kelly gang? And just where was it going to end?

He swallowed as his line of vision shifted to the spread of new light beyond the batwings. Sun-up was close.

He stifled a shiver.

Myram Casey brandished a flaring match at the cigar clamped between his teeth, lit it and blew a line of smoke as if drawing a discreet curtain across the scene below him. Not that it was anything new. Only the setting was different. The sight of a half-dozen naked girls bathing was part of the business. But at this time, in this place, it was dangerous.

He waited for the smoke to clear before calling to the girls. 'You ain't here on a mornin' picnic. Cut out the noise. No splashin', and no gigglin'. We don't want half the territory turnin' up for a show. Just get on with it.'

He blew another line of smoke and gazed anxiously around him. Place was remote enough – a hidden turn in the creek where the flow of shallow water had not yet dried up – deep within boulders, some stragglings of growth, a parched tree here and there and little else save dirt and rock. Doc had been right: 'Can't deny the girls their bathin' if that's what they're askin'. I spotted a creek that might suit. Get them there at sun-up and back within the hour. No messin'.'

Myram grunted quietly to himself, glanced quickly at the girls and went back to his watchful scanning of the surroundings. His thoughts strayed without any prompting: back to Firebow, to the Palace, the Kelly gang and whatever disgusting damage they had done to the place; to his present predicament living like a two-bit drifter under wagon canvas, eating sand and drinking dirt, trying best he could to keep his bar girls happy and fretting something rotten on his prospects. Not good, he had already decided, not unless the Kellys got to having second thoughts about Firebow and pulled out to lusher haunts.

But, damnit, how long was he supposed to survive out here, living like this? Doc was doing his best – a good job when you came to it – and the townsfolk's morale was holding steady, but there would come a day. . . .

The girls' laughter broke across his reverie as he turned sharply to call to them again. 'Get yourselves ready to move. Time we headed back. You hear me down there?'

The laughter ceased abruptly. The girls fell silent, unmoving with the water flowing freely around their legs, their gazes fixed on something downstream, out of Myram's line of vision. 'What's goin' on down there?' snapped Myram, clamping the cigar between his teeth. 'I said—'

'There's somebody here, Mr Casey,' said one of the girls without looking at Myram. 'Right here. Down there in the water. Just watchin'.'

Myram clouded himself in a swirl of smoke. 'What do you mean, somebody there? He one of us? One of the townsfolk?'

'No, Mr Casey, he ain't no townsman,' said the girl, her lips beginning to quiver.

Myram heeled the cigar angrily. 'You gals get yourselves dressed right now. You hear me? Get to it!'

The girls were beginning to shiver in spite of the

fierce sunlight and balmy air, their arms hugged across their breasts, their eyes bulging on the figure downstream.

'I don't think the fella wants us to do that, Mr Casey,' spluttered a girl with long yellow hair and pale-blue eyes. 'He's got a gun, a rifle, and I sure as hell reckon for him usin' it if he's a mind.'

'Well, I'll soon see about that,' growled Myram, drawing a bone-handled Colt from his gunbelt. 'You just wait right there.'

'No, mister, you just wait right where you are and drop that piece,' came a voice at Myram's back, followed by the slow, deliberate click of a gun hammer.

CHAPTER TEN

The sweat beaded hot and sticky on Myram Casey's brow. He dropped the Colt to the dirt at his feet and half turned to face the man at his back. 'Who in hell—' he began, only for his words to drown in his throat at the sudden piercing scream of one of the girls in the creek stream.

'Mr Casey,' sobbed another girl.

Myram squirmed and sweated. 'Who are you?' he mouthed drily.

'Chad Kelly,' said the man, a slow grin cracking his weathered face. 'And that's my brother Bonehead down there.'

Myram gulped. 'If you harm my girls—' he began again.

Kelly's grin broadened to a mocking smile. 'Bonehead,' he called, 'you go easy down there, you hear? Stop feastin' your eyes and get them gals dressed and ready to move. You can have all you like of 'em when we get back to town.'

'Just like you say, Brother,' answered Bonehead. 'Just like you say.'

Kelly turned his attention back to Myram. 'Now let me figure this,' he sneered, his eyes gleaming. 'You must be Myram Casey, owner of the Palace at Firebow, and them girls. Says so over the 'wings. Right?'

Myram swallowed. 'All I'm sayin—'

'You ain't sayin' nothin', mister, save to tell me how you got here. Let me figure again: a wagon and hitched team. Right? O'course I am. So we'll go get it, eh, and get them gals aboard and then we can all go back to town, can't we?'

'You ain't goin' to get away with this, mister,' groaned Myram. 'Not no how you ain't. There's folk—'

'Sure, sure,' quipped Kelly. 'A whole townload of 'em, eh? All back there in them rocks; all skulking clear of the Kelly boys. Quite right too. The Kellys don't take one snitch kindly to cowards. Nossir. So them folk had best stay where they are. We've got the girls and that'll do for now.' He took a step forward for a view of the stream. 'Them gals ready, Bonehead?'

'Fresh as spring and twice as tasty, Brother.'

'Well, get them up here fast. We've got a wagon waitin'.' He faced Myram. 'You're comin' with us, mister. Oh, yes. Somebody is goin' to get a rough surprise when you don't get back to the townsfolk, ain't they? You bet!'

The sweat on Myram's brow beaded again and trickled down his cheeks to the corners of his mouth and into his neck. He could already see the look on Doc Parker's face, hear the groans of the other men when they figured what had happened.

Hell, he thought, and all because the girls had wanted to bathe.

Maloney had wasted no time in leaving the store-room at the rear of the Palace and returning to the dusty room above the old saddlery. His entry to the bar and return to the hideout had by now become familiar and perfected, and a deal easier since Kelly's remaining sidekicks had shown no enthusiasm for investigating the rest of the deserted town. While ever they had the bar, the booze and the stolen money within sight, they were content to wait for their leader to plan the future.

Elmore, however, had no inclination, it seemed, to set about tracking down the whereabouts in town of the mysterious Marshal Carew. He had ordered that the men stay in the bar until Chad and Bonehead returned from their explorations. 'We ain't goin' no place now, not 'til them brothers of mine are back,' he had growled, through a thickening haze of the cheap whiskey Myram had left behind. 'Carew can wait. He wants to step through them batwings, and meet his Maker, that's his affair. I'll be waitin'. . . .'

The morning had grown hotter, the silence deeper; even the flies had gone to sleep. Only occasionally had Maloney stirred at the window to keep watch on a sidekick venturing tentatively through the 'wings to the boardwalk, and then for no more than a minute to catch whatever cleaner air there might be and glance quickly the length of the street for any signs of Carew.

There were never any, nor would there be, thought the sheriff. Carew was not the sort for showing himself without cause. Even so, what had he made of there being at least one townsman left in Firebow? Maloney was still wearing his badge of law. Had Carew seen it in the brief moment they had been within hailing distance of each other? Would he try to make contact, or would he simply wait? He was a patient man.

Another hour had passed before Maloney's thoughts strayed back again to Sam and his ride to Bottom Creek. The livery owner would not linger any longer than necessary with Doc Parker and the others. He would report the situation, repeat the warnings to stay clear, and then hightail it back again to within sight of Firebow before he hitched his mount some place and crept back to the saddlery.

That had been the plan, but Maloney was beginning to feel the first qualms of doubt as noon approached, the heat and silence thickened and there was still no sign of Sam. Damn it, any one of a dozen things could have gone wrong. Chad Kelly and his brother could have reached Bottom Creek and found Doc's encampment; they could have crossed Sam on his return ride; they could still be out there. Sam could be lying dead in some godforsaken, fly-infested gully.

But if Maloney was having qualms about Sam's fate, they were as nothing to the chill he felt at the sight of an approaching dust cloud far down the trail. Its progress was too slow to be riders, he decided, pressing as close to the window as he dared. That was a wagon, heading directly into Firebow.

The sound of it, the creaks and groans of hard-pressed timbers, the grind of wheels, crack of a whip and steady beat of hoofs, brought Kelly and his sidekicks to the boardwalk the minute the wagon reached the street.

'Look yuh here, fellas!' yelled Bonehead, swishing the whip through the air as he reined the outfit to a grinding halt at the saloon. 'Just feast your eyes on the lovelies we rounded up back there.'

The waiting men peered through the swirl of dust at the girls seated in the wagon under the protective glare of Myram Casey. 'Any man so much as lays a finger on these gals. . . .' he began, only to be silenced by Bonehead's crack of the whip across his back.

The girls cowered, shuddered, plucked nervously at their skimpy clothes, and stared like wide-eyed, dust-smeared fledglings into the slavering faces watching them.

'Whole town's holed-up out there,' said Chad, slipping from his lathered mount. 'These got careless.'

The men pressed closer as the dust cleared. 'The redhead's mine,' leered a sidekick already reaching for the shoulder of the girl nearest to him.

'Get them off the street and inside,' growled

Elmore Kelly, stepping through the batwings in a flurry of swirling dust-coat. 'You hear me – off the street. Right now.'

The sidekicks manhandled the girls from the wagon to the boardwalk, bustled them through the batwings and into the saloon.

'Easy, Brother, easy,' soothed Chad. 'Ain't no gun goin' to spit with them gals in its sights. That's the whole idea of bringin' 'em in. We got real lucky.'

'Mebbe,' said Elmore, his gaze taking in the street as if expecting it to come alive with levelled guns, 'but I ain't trustin' to Carew gettin' all gentlemanly because of a handful of gals.' His gaze settled on Chad. 'You learn anythin'?'

'That hotel proprietor ain't been slow to talk. Seems like the town got to hear of our comin' and pulled out to some creek. I don't figure for them bein' no trouble. They'll stay put in spite of the girls. Point is, we've got our edge and we can use it anytime, any which way we choose.' Chad wiped the dirt from his face. 'Best let the boys get to the gals, eh? Make up some for losin' their partners.'

The gang leader took a long, last look down the street. 'But we stay sharp. Carew ain't left town.'

Maloney eased away from the window, the sweat dripping from his chin to his stained shirt, his thoughts now in a swirl of uncertainties.

The Kellys were no longer in any doubt about what had happened to the townsfolk, but would they – now down to ten-strong – make any attempt to stage a raid on Bottom Creek? Doc and the others would guess soon enough what had befallen Casey and the girls. Would they decide on a move to mount some attempt at a rescue? God, he prayed not. That would be riding to a bloodbath.

What would be Carew's reaction to the taking of the girls? How safe an edge would they be for the gang? The Kellys would have no qualms in exploiting them to the full.

The sheriff paced the stifling storeroom; window to wall, wall to window. He pondered, his thoughts tumbling like loose rocks. What of Sam? Should he ride out to join him at the creek? Should he slip away from the saddlery now while the gang were occupied with the girls, and go hunt down Carew? Damn it, the fellow had to be somewhere.

He turned again at the wall, walked towards the window, but stopped halfway across the bare, dusty boards at the sound of a girl's high-pitched scream from somewhere deep in the saloon.

The sweat beaded again and dripped from Maloney's chin.

CHAPTER ELEVEN

'That's all we needed, as if there ain't enough to fret to.' Doc Parker tossed the dregs of a mug of coffee to the dust and pushed the band of his hat clear of his sticky brow. 'Might've known. Should have seen it comin'. Should never have let Casey take them girls to the creek. But, hell, what's a fella supposed to do?'

Doc stared forlornly into Sam Carr's eyes, replaced the mug on the makeshift camp table and finally raised a weak smile as he slapped the livery owner on the shoulder. 'Anyhow, good to see you. Glad you made it, not that the news is good from any angle.'

'You can say that again,' frowned Sam, making another effort to dust the trail dirt from his shirt. 'Ain't nothin' goin' for us right now, unless you count that mystery Marshal Carew as an edge. But who is he? Where is he? Do we find him, or leave him to his own devices, whatever they may be? Sheriff can't say, and neither can I. All I do know is that now, with the girls and Myram taken, we've got to do somethin'. Any thoughts?'

'We could raise enough for a raid on the town,' piped a man from the watching gathering. 'Most here can handle a piece. Can't leave the gals to the Kellys, that's for sure.'

'Bloodbath,' croaked an old-timer, smacking his lips. 'Nothin' short of it. Them Kelly guns are deadly. They don't miss. And, anyhow, they'd like as not shoot the gals first. We wouldn't be doin' them no favours.'

The men murmured and nodded.

'So, do we just leave 'em to their fate?' asked Doc, readjusting his hat. 'T'ain't much of an alternative, is it?'

Sam lit a thin cheroot and blew smoke. 'Let me take two men back to town,' he said, examining the glow of the tip. 'Two of our best shots. That'd make us four strong, plus Carew if we can make contact. That way we might be able to do somethin' constructive. Ain't quite sure what, but we sure as hell can't risk puttin' a whole town's manhood at risk. That would be madness.' He drew on the cheroot again and blew more smoke. 'So who's it to be? Make up your minds. We leave inside the hour.'

Myram Casey jumped to his feet from the chair in the corner of the smoke-laden saloon bar, his face glowing with sweat and anger as one of Kelly's sidekicks dragged a struggling girl towards the stairs to the upper storey rooms. 'I said no rough handlin' of my girls,' he protested. 'Ain't allowed, not on these premises it ain't.'

The sidekick halted, glared, tightened his grip on the girl's arm and with his right hand, drew a Colt from his low-slung holster. 'You want I should shut this rat's mouth, Elmore?' he growled, glancing quickly at the gang leader. 'He's gettin' awful irritatin' with that lip of his.'

'He lives. We need him,' said Kelly without turning from his watch on the street from the batwings. 'Sit down, Casey. You ain't in charge here no more,' he added.

Myram stood his ground, his anger stiffening his body ramrod straight. 'You ain't goin' to get away with none of this, Kelly,' he fumed. 'You'll see. It'll happen. They'll be here to get you. You see if I ain't right.'

Kelly turned from the batwings. 'And just who might *they* be, mister? You tell me.'

'I ain't sayin' no more,' said Myram haughtily. 'You just wait and see. Longer you're here the worse—'

'Sit down!' bellowed Kelly. 'And stay quiet. One more word out of you and I'll have my Bonehead there take you apart, limb by limb. So sit, and don't move.'

Myram backed to the chair and sat down again. Kelly turned to his watch from the 'wings, and the sneering sidekick headed for the stairs with the girl in tow.

Bonehead, standing guard over the other girls, cracked his knuckles and smiled with a grunt of satisfaction. 'I ain't had me a haul of females like this since them days way back at Bakerstown. You remember them days, Chad?'

Chad Kelly tested the sharpness of his knife blade against the tip of his finger, glanced at the clutch of cowering girls, and shrugged. 'I seen better,' he murmured. 'But I ain't fussed none. They ain't worth more than their bargainin' use. Ain't that so, Elmore?'

'S'right,' answered Kelly from the wings. 'That's all they're worth. Just enough to force Carew to show his miserable face – which, at the moment, he ain't exactly rushin' to do.'

'Mebbe we should get to promptin' him,' said one of the sidekicks sauntering across the bar to Elmore's side. 'Show him what we mean, what we're about and we ain't soft on doin' it.'

'Mebbe you're right at that, my friend,' said Elmore. 'Mebbe we should get to showin' the way of things.'

Chad slid the blade to its sheath and poured himself a drink. 'How about the proprietor here? We could string him up. Hang him slow, right there in the street.'

'He ain't goin' to be no loss. Not with that lip of his he ain't,' agreed Bonehead, running his fingers over a girl's bare shoulder. 'So what say we do it? Right now.'

Myram squirmed uncomfortably, the sweat flowing freely down his cheeks, but he held his silence. The girls cowered closer, their eyes wide and wild, their throats as dry as trail dust.

'How soon before them townsfolk show their faces?' asked a taller, leaner gunslinger, sprawling his weight across the bar. 'They ain't goin' to take to the loss of the gals lyin' down, are they? Ain't goin' to sit out there doin' nothin'.'

Another sidekick murmured his agreement. 'Supposin' they ride in, guns blazin' like it's jubilation day or somethin'?'

'Suppose they do,' shrugged Bonehead, 'then we shoot 'em, every last one. Won't be no trouble. There ain't a gun between here and the Rockies the Kelly boys can't silence. Ain't that a fact, Elmore?'

'If you reckon so, Brother.' Elmore moved across the batwings, his eyes narrowed and tight in their scan of the street and its buildings. 'But mebbe there's another way.' He scratched the nape of his neck. 'Yeah, mebbe there is.' He swung round abruptly. 'We'll go find Carew for ourselves. Search the town, one end to the other, missin' nothin'. And the girls and that lippy proprietor will be our shield.'

'Now we're gettin' somewhere,' grinned Bonehead. 'We'll have Carew flushed through in no time. What you reckon, Chad?'

Chad Kelly merely smiled and adjusted the set of his gunbelt. 'Somebody go rouse that sonofabitch upstairs. And bring the girl. We want 'em all on show.'

They had assembled the girls and Casey on the boardwalk fronting the bar, when the sidekick sent to fetch his partner and the girl from the hotel room, pushed through the batwings, a look of shock and disbelief on his face.

'He's dead,' he croaked, as if the words were stones in his throat. 'Frank's dead. Stabbed. Carew must've been waitin' on him. Up there all the time.'

The sidekicks simply stared then turned to look at Elmore Kelly whose ruddy colour had faded suddenly to an ashen grey. 'Where's the girl?' he growled.

'She ain't there. She's gone,' said the man.

'What do you mean gone?' growled Kelly again.

'Just that – gone. Carew must have taken her.'

Myram Casey sheltered a girl against him. Bonehead swallowed and wiped his sweat-soaked neck. Chad Kelly moved slowly to the steps to the street and gazed over the darkened rows of doors and windows facing him. 'He's out there,' he murmured. 'He's got the edge again, damn him.'

'Inside,' rasped Elmore. 'All of you. Back inside. Shift it!'

CHAPTER TWELVE

Elmore Kelly closed the door on the body of the dead sidekick and took a slow step into the shadows of the balcony above the saloon bar. He half turned to face his brothers, but said nothing.

Bonehead fidgeted from one foot to the other, his fingers sliding nervously over the butt of his holstered Colt. 'Three dead,' he muttered, as if to himself. 'Just like that. Easy as throwin' pebbles in a pool.' He hooked his thumbs in his belt. 'Carry on like this and there won't be nobody standin' inside a week.'

'Shut that talk,' spat Elmore.

'Shut it maybe,' said Bonehead. 'Simple enough, Brother, but you can't sidestep the truth that easy. Ask Chad here. Ask the boys down there. Booze and gals is one thing; dead partners is another. Only so much they'll take, specially when it's Carew doin' the killin'.'

'He's got a point there,' agreed Chad, gazing into the bar below him where the smoke haze hung like a shroud over the silent sidekicks and bar girls. 'The boys'll be for pullin' out and puttin' this town behind 'em. T'ain't brought them a deal save death. Mebbe we should listen to 'em.'

Bonehead nodded. 'I'm for that. Let's put it to 'em: we pull out under cover of night and ride south. Hell, we've got enough money to buy us whatever takes our fancy. We don't have to be holed up in a two-bit ghost town. Even take some of the girls if we've a mind.'

'Carew will follow,' grunted Elmore.

'So let him,' shrugged Bonehead. 'Mebbe next time he catches up things'll be different.'

'Sure,' grunted Elmore again, 'like havin' a whole posse of lawmen along of him. Carew ain't for givin' up, not now he's come this far, and not now he's makin' a move. He'll be there, just like he always is, just like he's always been.' He took a few steps deeper into the shadows and stared into space. 'We walk away from him now and he'll haunt us forever.'

'Could say he's doin' that already,' mumbled Chad.

Elmore turned slowly. 'Remember, we planned back there after the raid that we'd settle with Carew once and for all. Get him off our backs. And this is our chance. The best we've ever had. There won't be another. So there'll be no ridin' south, and no talk of it neither.' His stare hardened and darkened. 'Now get me one of them girls. I'm goin' to give Carew a message.'

Maloney listened, straining for the slightest sound, the softest movement. There had been one sure

enough, soon after Kelly and the gang had shepherded the bar girls back to the saloon from the
boardwalk. Had it been a step, more than one? A
shuffle of steps, somewhere out there on the stairs
from the old saddlery shop to the storeroom?

He had taken a look, but there had been nothing to see, nothing to hear save the buzzing of a
lost fly. He had come back to the window but
continued to feel the strange closeness of a presence. Maybe it was Carew. Maybe he was making
his move. And not before time. Another day of
being cooped up in this sweat-box of a room. . . .

Hold it, there was a burst of activity in the street.

Elmore Kelly had pushed through the batwings,
one of the girls held tight across him, a Colt
levelled menacingly close to her temple. He
paused a moment on the boardwalk, glanced to
left and right, then bustled the girl down the steps
and into the searing glare of the street.

The girl stood near lifeless in the man's grip, too
scared to murmur a sound, barely to blink, her
eyes wide and round and filled with fear. Kelly
tightened the hold across her breasts, settled the
barrel of the Colt at her head, and gazed around
him.

'I'm goin' to say this only once, Carew,' he
bellowed, across the flat, heat-hazed air. 'There
won't be no repeatin' it, so you listen up real good,
eh, wherever you're skulkin' like the rat you are.'

The girl swallowed, almost lost her footing
under her trembling legs and seemed for a second
to be staring directly into Maloney's eyes where he

watched from the side of the window in the store-room.

'Like you can see, Carew, me and the boys have gotten ourselves a handful of hostages: the girls and the owner of this two-bit hotel. Seems like you've taken one of the gals for yourself. So be it. Enjoy her. Don't make no odds to the proposition I got.'

Maloney frowned at the news of one of the girls being with Carew. Where? How? What was he planning?

Kelly's voice was booming out again. 'Here's the deal: we settle this once and for all. You show your-self and you and me will shoot it out. No more takin' out my men like some rattler slitherin' in and out of its nest. All right? Now, if you don't go along with my proposition, I promise you on my very breath that I'll start killin' these girls one at a time, every hour on the hour. You've got 'til midnight tonight to do as I say.' He waited a moment. 'I know you for a thinkin' fella, Carew. You ain't nobody's fool, and I don't figure for you takin' me for one neither. So let's do this sensible and civilized, eh? Remember – midnight.'

Kelly had dragged the girl back to the boardwalk and through the batwings in seconds, leaving no more than the scuffed dirt of the street and its shimmering drift of dust.

Maloney eased clear of the window and stared at the Winchester propped against the storeroom wall. Maybe he should have risked a shot at Kelly.

Maybe he would have got lucky. Sure, he thought, and that shot would have brought the whole of the Kelly gang rampaging into the street like a whirlwind. And no accounting for the deaths and destruction that would have followed.

He wiped the sweat from his neck and face and went back to pacing the room – window to wall, wall to window.

His mind raced. There was no chance Marshal Carew would go along with Kelly's proposition. The odds would be stacked against him from the start, with a primed gun waiting at every window, in every doorway, on every rooftop the minute he stepped into the street.

But would Kelly carry out his threat? Had he the stomach for the cold-blooded murder of the girls? Maloney had slowed his pacing only briefly in the realization that Elmore Kelly and his brothers, and doubtless the rest of the bunch, were capable of and would carry out the killings without a second thought.

He turned at the wall and stopped dead in his tracks. The sound was there again. Closer now. Outside the door to the room. No more than a slow, soft step. He waited, easing round to face the door at his side; drew his Colt, tightened the grip.

The doorknob turned as if touched by a nervous child. Maloney swallowed and sweated. He dared not risk a shot. The Kellys would discover the storeroom. He would have to rely on a fast attack with the barrel of the pistol, keeping it as sudden and quiet as possible.

He swallowed again, blinked, licked at trickles of sweat and watched, his eyes narrowed, as the door eased open slowly.

He had grabbed the girl and dragged her into the room before she had taken her next breath.

'What the—?' he croaked, swinging the startled girl around as he leaned back to close the door. She gasped and fought to find her voice. 'Sheriff Maloney . . . thank God,' she finally groaned, pushing back her hair then trying best as she could to pull her torn dress into shape across her body. 'I never thought. . . .'

'Easy there,' urged Maloney, steadying the girl as she swayed uncertainly on her feet. 'Best sit down. Sorry there ain't nowhere but the floor. Easy now.'

The girl sank to a sitting position, closed her eyes for a moment, then managed a faint smile. 'Thanks. I sure am glad to see you.'

'What happened? How did you get out of the saloon? Take your time. Tell me in your words.' He looked closer at the girl. 'You're Alice, aren't you?'

'S'right, Mr Maloney. Me and the other girls and Mr Casey were bushwhacked by them Kelly brothers out at the creek stream. Don't know whether the townfolk know what happened, but I guess they'll figure it soon enough.' Alice pushed at her hair again and wiped the beading sweat from her neck. 'One of them scum grabbed me and took me to a room. But that was as far as the rat got. Minute he'd closed the door and made another grab for me, there was a sudden movement from the corner and this man – Carew he said his name was, Marshal Carew – sprang out and knifed the fella faster than you could blink.'

The girl shuddered in spite of the oppressive heat of the storeroom. 'We left the sidekick and disappeared down the back stairs into them old shacks back of the Palace. I was too dazed to know what was happening, but the marshal seemed sure enough. He said as how he knew you and another man had stayed in town and were holed up above the saddlery. He would take me there but I was to wait long enough for him to be away again before making contact with you.'

'Did he say where he was goin'?' asked Maloney.

'No, he just said to tell you as how he'd be around. Just that, then he left; drifted away like a shadow. He's a cool customer and no mistake, Mr Maloney. Kinda scary in a way, all them dark clothes and twin Colts, but he sure ain't got no time for the Kelly gang. You bet he ain't. What's he planning, do you know? And what we going to do about the girls and Mr Casey? Did you hear what Kelly threatened? Believe me, he'll do it, too. You can see it in his eyes. He hates that Marshal Carew, really hates him, deep down so that it gnaws at him like something bad and festering.'

Alice shivered. 'We're going to have to think of something, Mr Maloney, 'cos if we don't this town will be running with blood.'

79

CHAPTER THIRTEEN

It had taken Sam and the two townsmen chosen to ride with him until well into the hours of darkness before they had finally summoned the nerve to approach Firebow and make the bid to reach the saddlery.

'No point in hurryin' things,' Sam had reasoned, once they had the dark, empty street and the looming bulks of the buildings in their sights from the cover of the rock outcrop a quarter-mile or so from town. 'We ride as close as we dare to that old barn of mine back of the livery. There's food and water for the horses and a safe hitch line well out of the sight of the Kelly boys. We head for the saddlery on foot. Just follow me.'

Hank Forman and Joe Burns had simply nodded, tapped their holstered Colts and the stocks of their Winchesters, and settled their grip on already shortened reins. 'No problem,' young Hank had murmured through his flashing grin. 'Let's get to Maloney fast as we can.'

'But no heroics,' Joe had urged, tipping the brim of his hat. 'We know how handy you are with

80

them shooters, Hank, but there's a time and place. Right now gettin' unseen into town is the priority. That so, Sam?'

'To the hilt,' said Sam. 'I ain't sure what it is we're goin' to be able to do, but I'm darn certain Sheriff Maloney is goin' to be pleased to see us. And mebbe he's managed to make contact with Carew. Meantime, remember the girls and Casey bein' held in there. They ain't got no options save to sit it out and pray. It's them we've got to stay aware of. No lettin' 'em down, eh?'

They had ridden on like shadows.

Myram Casey sweated somewhere in the confusion between near exhaustion and seething impatience. He wanted to do something, anything. But what, and did he have the strength or, come to that, the know-how?

He glanced round his once sparkling, bustling bar where now the smoky air lay thick as mist and the smells of liquor and human bodies seemed to hang like an impenetrable shroud. The lights were primed to their lowest, the silence something you could touch.

Elmore Kelly sat alone as ever in a shadowed corner of the bar, a bottle of whiskey and a glass on the table in front of him, his mood dark and brooding, his stare fixed on a space and images only he could see. How long, wondered Myram on a deep swallow, before he retreated from his thoughts and raised his eyes to watch the bar clock tick round to midnight? Would he carry out his threat? Had he the stomach for it – the cold-blooded shooting of innocent women?

He had, thought Myram, and probably a whole sight worse if it came to it.

Chad Kelly had positioned himself close to the batwings within sight of the street and the facing windows. He, more than anyone, seemed aware of the danger in Carew's presence in town and the stranglehold he had on movement. There was not one of the gang who would dare now to step into the street alone or make a move anywhere beyond the bar.

Nor, pondered Myram, with almost a wry smile to himself, were they aware of Maloney being holed up some place. Had he and Carew made contact? Was Alice with the sheriff? What of Doc and the townsfolk out at Bottom Creek? And what—?

His tumbling thoughts were broken by the crack of Bonehead's voice.

'What say we liven things up round here?' he grinned, slapping the shoulders of one of the girls. 'Give ourselves a party night, eh? Heck, we got the booze, we got the girls. Damn it, we've got a whole town!'

Pairs of tired eyes lazed to look at him through the gloom. Chad Kelly merely half turned to him; Elmore paid him no attention.

'Bet your life we've got some dancin' girls here,' Bonehead began again, dragging one of the girls to her feet. 'How about that!' He twirled the girl away from him. She stumbled. Myram rose to his feet. 'Dance, damn you!' yelled Bonehead, drawing his Colt.

'Put that gun down, Brother, else I'll kill you m'self, so help me God I will,' growled Elmore from the corner.

Bonehead shrugged and holstered the Colt. Myram lowered himself slowly to his chair. The girl joined the others and shuddered in their protective closeness.

'Easy, little Brother, easy,' urged Chad, still watching the street from the 'wings. 'This ain't no time for a hoedown. We ain't in the mood. You should be showin' some respect for our dead partners.'

'They took their chance same as the rest of us,' sulked Bonehead, pouring himself a hefty drink. 'We all take the chance. Always have. Elmore himself said so. Whole darn business is a chance, ain't that so, boys?' He sank the drink in one noisy gulp.

A rangy, lean-limbed sidekick idled to his feet from a nearby table. 'Me and the boys have been thinkin' on some,' he drawled, glancing quickly at the brooding bulk of Elmore. 'Got to reckonin' on the future from here on in. Not that we ain't with you, boss. We are, all the way, just like you've always said. But time's tickin' on and we ain't exactly makin' any mark round here, are we? I mean—'

'Why don't you get to the point, fella,' snapped Chad without turning from his vigil. 'Say what's on your mind. We're listenin', ain't we, Elmore?'

Kelly grunted from his corner table and poured

a measure of whiskey to the glass.

The rangy sidekick shifted his feet, glanced at his anxious colleagues, but avoided the hawkish stare of Elmore. 'We just figure there's mebbe somethin' to be said for pullin' out of this two-bit dump right now. Tonight. While it's dark. Hell, we got money enough to head any which way we fancy. Could take some liquor along of us, and mebbe a couple of the girls here. We could be clean through to the open plains again before sun-up; ridin' south before noon, or west again if we've a mind. Or mebbe have ourselves some good times in one of them fancy towns back East. I heard say there ain't nothin' a man could want for in one of them towns. How about that?' The man paused, his cheeks flushed, the sweat beading, his eyes like marbles in syrup. 'Still, choice would be yours, boss, just like it's always been. We ain't for messin' none and, damn it, we've come—'

'Know somethin', fella,' said Elmore, his voice grinding out the words. 'I reckon you may have a point there.'

'You do?' smiled the sidekick. 'Hear that, boys?'

'Sure, I do,' said Elmore, pouring another measure. 'Why not? Like you say, time's tickin' on, and who wants a ghost town, anyhow? So I figure we might do as you say.'

Chad Kelly smiled softly to himself. Bonehead frowned. Myram Casey's thoughts whirled as if caught in a plains' wind. The girls simply stared.

'Well, now—' began the sidekick, rubbing his hands together.

'You go fetch the horses,' growled Elmore, his eyes darkening. 'Now.'

'You bet,' said the man. 'Me and Mel here—'

'Alone. You go fetch the horses alone.' Kelly's stare was unblinking.

'But, I—'

'Do it,' ordered Elmore, slopping whiskey as he crashed the glass to the table.

The sidekick hesitated, wiped the sweat from his face, settled his hat and hitched his pants. 'You got it, boss,' he murmured, crossing to the batwings.

Chad Kelly stood aside for him and smiled as the fellow passed through the wings to the boardwalk. He stood for a moment, glancing to left, to right as if expecting the night to part for him, and had taken a step towards the street when the single shot rang out at his back.

It was some seconds before he tried to move, a look of blank amazement on his face, his lips twitching, his mind willing a suddenly numbed body to turn to see whose finger had been on the trigger. But all he ever saw was a wisp of gunsmoke trailing like a last breath into the night. Then he fell and did not move again.

Chad Kelly holstered his Colt and closed the batwings on a slow, mournful creak.

CHAPTER
FOURTEEN

'In the back,' murmured Sam, turning from the storeroom window. 'Point blank. Cold, cowardly killin'. There ain't no other way to say it.'

Sheriff Maloney leaned back on the wall, mopped the sweat from his neck and peered through the gloom at the grey silent faces watching him. 'Only reckonin' to our advantage is when they get to shootin' their own we've mebbe got some hope.'

Joe Burns had nodded his agreement; Hank Forman had paced the room again and crashed a fist to the palm of his hand; Alice had closed her eyes and wished for the hundredth time she had stayed back home with the ranch-house chores.

'Why?' asked Joe. 'Why have they come to this? They fallin' out over the money or somethin'?'

'It's all over who's for stayin' and who's for pullin' out would be my guess,' offered Sam. 'Some of them sidekicks have mebbe got to realizin' that Carew's got the edge right now. I'd figure for the one Chad Kelly's just shot as headin' for the livery to collect the horses. But the boss has no intention of ridin', not while Carew's still here. This is showdown time for Elmore Kelly and the mysterious Marshal Carew.'

'Mebbe I should go seek him out,' said Hank. 'Hell, them Kelly boys don't know to us yet. They think the only one in town is Carew. While they're all holed up there in the Palace, don't we have an edge? I'm for usin' it.'

Maloney pushed himself from the wall. 'And mebbe we'll do just that,' he said, peering through the window at the silent, shadow-filled street. 'Time we paid a visit to the Palace. Follow me, Hank, but keep your eyes peeled and your steps as soft as a fly's.'

Hank nodded, smiled and patted the butt of his holstered Colt.

'Give it an hour, then Joe and me will take over,' Carr offered. Let's see if there ain't some way we can get them girls out of Kelly's clutches.'

'My thinkin' precisely, Mr Carr,' winked Maloney. 'More trouble them rats have got, the thinner their patience.'

Alice opened her eyes with a start, but clasped her hands in silent prayer.

'That's the way of it: no pullin' out, no ridin' south or any place else for that matter. We're here, and so is Carew. We kill him, then we ride.' Elmore Kelly gulped a measure of whiskey, wiped his mouth with the back of his hand, and filled the glass again from a half-empty bottle. 'Any man here thinks other will finish up along of the rat out there. That clear?'

A sidekick stepped from the gloom to face the gang leader. 'That weren't necessary, Elmore. That was murderin' one of our own. We ain't never stooped to that before.' The sweat beaded like ice on his brow. 'The boys here ain't happy about it. Ain't no good reason to play into Carew's hands.' Kelly stayed silent, staring into the glass of whiskey. 'We figure on puttin' an end to it now.'

'And how do you propose doin' that?' asked Bonehead, from the bar. 'Clock's still tickin'. Carew will know the time. We don't need to do nothin'.'

'That's as mebbe.' The sidekick glanced at the bar clock. 'If we ain't for ridin',' there ain't nothin' to stop us gettin' face-on to Carew. We're all agreed – we get out there, right now, and we find Carew. Finish it. Then we split the money and ride, any place of our choosin'. Stayin' here, just waitin', killin' the women . . . that ain't no way. See that, don't you?'

'Oh, sure,' mocked Bonehead with a wild gesture. 'Sure. Just like the fella lyin' dead out there 'cus of his own stupidity. It's like we've said more times than a hound scratches fleas, we set a foot into that street and Carew will—'

'Hold it,' said Chad Kelly from his lookout at the batwings. 'There's a light.'

'A light?' echoed Bonehead. 'Where, f'Cris'sake?' He crossed to his brother's side. 'He's right. There is a light.'

88

Elmore Kelly came to his feet without a sound, a cigar glowing between his fingers. 'Get them girls to the back of the bar,' he ordered, glaring at Casey. 'And don't move 'til I say so.' He flicked his gaze to the sidekicks. 'One of you stay close to 'em. Shoot that bar owner if he so much as mutters.' Myram swallowed, sweated and croaked his whispered encouragement to the girls as he shepherded them into the deeper shadows.

'What do you see?' asked Elmore, stepping round the table. 'Where's the light comin' from?'

'Somewhere in the mercantile,' muttered Bonehead.

'That ain't Carew,' said Chad, peering into the night at the faint glow of light in the left-hand window of the store. 'He wouldn't be that stupid.'

'Mebbe it's the bar girl he snaffled away,' offered Bonehead, one hand already closing its grip on the butt of his Colt. 'Mebbe she's gotten careless.'

'Let me go take a look,' said a sidekick, easing his way to the 'wings. 'This is mebbe the chance we've been waitin' for.'

'Stay where you are!' bellowed Elmore Kelly, coming to the centre of the bar. 'You set a foot on that boardwalk and you're a dead man.'

The sidekick halted and turned slowly to face Kelly. 'So what do you suggest?' he sneered.

'Use the back door. Slip out that way and work round to the street. But no shootin'. See what you can see and get back, fast. Go.'

The sidekick nodded and slid away.

'The rest of you—'

The night filled suddenly with a cracking, whining spray of rifle fire from the street that ripped into the timbers of Casey's saloon like a snort of flame.

Shards of shattered glass and splinters of wood sprayed across the room in a shower of deadly barbs. Two sidekicks fell back, one dead instantly, the other bleeding heavily from a chest wound. Bonehead sprawled full length as if pole-axed, his curses ringing like growls of thunder; Chad Kelly had pressed himself to a far wall, a Colt bristling uselessly in his grip. Elmore Kelly prowled catlike at the back of the bar, sweat beading and glistening on his face, his eyes as fiery as coals.

A girl had screamed but fallen silent at the slap of Casey's hand across her mouth. Now she huddled with the others in the shadows, fearful of closing her eyes on the mayhem around her, too scared not to, but like Casey, unaware of the door behind her opening slowly.

CHAPTER FIFTEEN

'They've gone, every last one, includin' that cringin' owner. Out through the back door. So who was there, eh? Somebody was. Somebody got them out and away. Couldn't have been Carew. He was too busy blastin' us to hell from the street. So if it wasn't Carew, it was somebody workin' with him. An accomplice. He's got help, damn him!'

Elmore Kelly scuffed his boot through shards of glass, aimed a stream of spittle at a spittoon, and missed. 'Hell,' he cursed, and kicked the leg of a broken chair into a pool of drying blood. 'And two more dead,' he added through a grunt.

'Place is cursed,' said Bonehead, slumped at a table, a newly opened bottle of whiskey gloating at him. 'Has been all along. Minute we set foot in it. That's Carew's doin'. Him and . . . So who in hell could be workin' with him?'

Chad Kelly strolled casually from the shadows to the side of the batwings. 'Somebody who knew about the back door, where it led and how you could spirit a line of snivellin' bar girls through it and out of sight. Somebody who's been watchin' us since we got here.' He turned to face his brothers. 'A "somebody" who has taken our edge and trapped us.'

A sidekick ran a bandanna round his neck. 'We ain't never been trapped. Nobody would have the stomach for it.'

'Until now,' said Chad, turning back to the batwings. He moved closer to scan the street, where the first light of the new day was beginning to break.

'All quiet out there now. Carew's restin' up. Ain't that a consolin' thought!'

'We were right – we should've pulled out long back,' muttered a sidekick, pouring himself a large drink and sinking it in one deep gulp. 'Six dead. Six . . . Who'd have rated it? Six dead and we ain't fired a decent shot in days. So who's next, Elmore, you figured that? Tell you somethin', it ain't goin' to be me. I'm goin' to see to that. Suggest we all do the same.' He poured a second drink and sank it. 'Give it another hour 'til full light, then we pull out.'

'We get the girls back,' said Elmore, pacing into the shadows. 'That shouldn't be difficult. We get them – then we get Carew.'

'Forget Carew,' snapped the sidekick. 'Leave him. We can slip away, hit the trail, be long gone by noon. And if Carew wants to follow, let him. We'll deal with him some place else. Some place where we've got the edge again.'

The other sidekicks murmured their agreement. 'Makes sense to me,' said one. 'Damn it, we've lost the girls. We ain't got nothin' to bargain with no more, so what we waitin' on? Let's ride.'

'Mebbe we should,' added Bonehead, still staring at the bottle of whiskey. 'Or mebbe we should torch this godforsaken town then go find them townsfolk and do the same to their wagons.'

A sidekick shifted his feet impatiently, 'Let's just split the money and go. Hell, if we leave here one at a time, headin' for wherever we got a fancy, Carew can't trail us all, can he? He can't be in two places at the same time.'

The sidekicks, Elmore Kelly and Bonehead fell silent as Chad, his back to them from his watch at the batwings, raised his right arm slowly. 'Well, now,' he murmured, 'what have we here?' He lowered his arm, gestured for complete silence and no movement, and eased softly to the right-hand side of the 'wings. 'Yeah . . . Just as I thought. They're there. Holed up like hens in a coop.' He smiled softly to himself. 'Upstairs room at that old saddlery 'cross the street; a girl at the window. Nobody there now, but that's where they are, sure enough.' He turned, took a cheroot from his vest pocket, lit it and blew a drifting curl of smoke. 'We got 'em! Now let's do it!'

'Stand clear of that window.' Sheriff Maloney hissed the order through clenched teeth and stared hard as the red-faced bar girl backed to the wall of the stifling room and shivered in spite of the heat.

'Sorry,' said the girl, glancing guiltily at the others crowded into the shadowy confinement. 'Wasn't thinking.'

'Thinkin's about the only thing keepin' us alive round here,' muttered Maloney, taking up his familiar station at the side of the window. He glanced quickly into the street where the new light was spreading like something poured slowly. 'Them scum down there only need a half chance. So far we've been lucky, 'specially gettin' you clear like we did, but luck's a mite tricky hereabouts.' He smiled reassuringly at the girl, 'Don't worry, we'll have you out of here soon as we can.'

'Grateful for what you did back there, Maloney,' said Myram Casey, mopping an already sodden bandanna over his face. 'Took some guts to do what you did, but we made it; by God, we made it. Wouldn't like to see the look on Kelly's face right now. Or hear him, come to that!'

'It's Marshal Carew we should be thankin',' said Sam Carr, spinning the chamber of his Colt as he checked it for ammunition. 'That blast of firin' he let rip came just at the right time. Almost as if he knew.'

Casey flourished the bandanna. 'Mebbe he did.'

Hank Forman pushed himself clear of the door. 'What you sayin'? You figure for Carew watchin' us as well as the Kelly mob?'

'Well, mebbe he is at that,' said Casey. 'He knows we're here. He don't show himself, but, hell, he sure makes his presence felt. Ain't no arguin' to that.'

Joe Burns eased to Maloney's side. 'Question is: what's his next move? What's *our* next move come to that?'

'We get the girls back to Bottom Creek and safe with the others,' said Maloney.

'How? When? You got some plan?' asked Joe.

'The Kellys hitched that wagon and team back at Sam's livery. Somehow we've got to get the girls, Myram and yourself up there. Then you head for the creek and report to Doc. No stoppin'. Sam, myself and Hank stay here and try best we can to make contact with Carew, though frankly, I ain't got much hope of that.'

Sam holstered his Colt and came to the side of the window. He glanced quickly into the street to the silent, shadow-locked saloon. 'What's Kelly figurin' now? He goin' to pull out before he suffers any more losses, or will he still reckon on squarin' up to Carew? And just what's he figured has happened to the girls? They were his edge 'til the marshal got busy again.'

'Well, let's not give him the chance of findin' out,' blustered Casey, pocketing the bandanna as a new surge of sweat beaded across his brow. 'Let's get movin'.'

'Don't all leave together,' ordered Maloney. 'No more than two at a time. Use the back ways. And when you get to the livery, stay hidden. Don't get aboard the wagon 'til you're good and ready to pull out.'

*

The transfer of the girls from the room above the old saddlery to the livery began slowly, silently, nothing said, save in whispers, nothing rushed.

The six girls were shifted in three moves, each pair escorted through the shambles of outbuildings by Hank Forman. Once at the livery, they were led into hiding by Sam. 'We wait 'til you're all here, along of Joe and Myram, then I hitch the team, you load up and pull away to the trail. You'll be clear of town and out of sight in half an hour. And don't let me see you back here 'til we're good and ready!'

Alice was in the last pair to leave the saddlery. 'If – when – you see Carew again, will you tell him. . . .' she faltered. 'Yeah, well, I guess he knows. Me and the girls, we're all grateful to you and to him. It could all have—'

'Just get movin', will you?' Maloney had insisted. 'There ain't the time for talk. Tell Sam to stay where he is 'til he's satisfied you're clear of town. And you, Myram,' he had nodded to the Palace proprietor, 'you just make sure you stay put at the creek. With any luck, we might have this over in another couple of days. . . .'

Maloney was still watching anxiously at the saddlery window, the sweat coursing down his cheeks in salty streams, when the scurrying figure of Sam appeared from behind the rooming-house and ran hell-for-leather, arms waving into the street.

'What in the name of—' mouthed Maloney,

96

before blistering shouts filled the street like the echoes of haunting.

'For Cris'sake get down here, Sheriff, them Kelly scum have ridden out after the wagon!'

CHAPTER SIXTEEN

Maloney left the room, crashed down the stairs to the street to join Sam, a swirl of dust shimmering through a haze around him. 'What happened?' he croaked, wiping a hand across his mouth.

'Goddamnit, they must have been waitin',' wheezed Sam. 'The whole miserable bunch of 'em.' He gulped, his eyes watering against the intense glare. 'We had the wagon loaded, no trouble, Joe all set to drive, Casey ridin' shotgun. They left. Hank and me waited, watched. Hardly moved. It was all quiet – so we thought.' He paused a moment, took a deeper breath. 'Waited another five minutes, then the gang appeared, one by one; all saddled up, ready to ride, their eyes fixed like hawks on the trail Joe had just taken.'

'They see you?'

'Don't reckon so, but they'd been watchin', must've been. They'd reckoned on us makin' a bid to get the girls away. Now all they've got to do is follow 'til the outfit's clear down the trail, then . . . Hell, that don't bear thinkin' to.'

'Where's Hank?'

'Fetchin' the horses from the old barn.' Sam swallowed. 'We've got to ride, fast as we can. If Kelly. . . .' He spat and looked round the street. 'Any sign of that marshal, f'Cris'sake?' He cleared his throat and shouted at the top of his croaky voice. 'Carew, you here some place, 'cus if you are we sure as hell need your help right now.' The words echoed but fell into silence. 'Goddamnit,' mouthed Sam.

'No time for that,' urged Maloney. 'Let's get after that wagon.'

They rode fast and hard for the first mile, their eyes narrowed on the trail ahead, squinting against the swirl of dust, the skimming dirt, mouths dry, the scorch of the air like flame against their cheeks.

Maloney had already decided they would veer clear of the main trail at the point known locally as Stone Edge. 'The Kellys are too many guns for us to handle,' he had called to Sam and Hank. 'If we come off the trail at the Edge and keep up the pace we might get ahead of Joe, have time to warn him. It's the only thing we can do.'

They cleared Stone Edge in the next half-hour, heading at first through the cut of a narrow creek, then, as they came higher again, across flatter, open ground where the mounts responded instantly to the looser rein.

'Another half-mile,' shouted Maloney above the rush and bite of air, the beat of hoofs. 'There's a track twists through scrub back towards the trail.

Take that and we just might be in time—'

And then they heard the first crack and whine of gunfire.

The riders slithered and reined their mounts to a halt, the dust swirling about them like a grey-yellow mist.

'They've caught up, damn it,' cursed Sam. 'We're goin' to be too late.'

Gunfire cracked again. A man yelled. A girl screamed.

'We ain't doin' no good sittin' here,' groaned Hank, fighting to control his suddenly spooked horse. 'What's it to be: back to the main trail, or do we keep goin' to the track?'

'The track,' ordered Maloney. 'I ain't for presentin' them scum with a head-on target.'

They rode on, the whine and crack of more shots ringing in their ears as they crossed the flats and dropped again towards the matted straggle of brush and scrub. Maloney raised an arm to indicate the track ahead and led, slowing his pace, into the clinging growth.

Sam cursed and hacked at the dried fingers of brush with his bare hands. Hank kicked out to widen the tracks; Maloney simply pushed on, the sweat darkening his shirt, dripping from his chin, clouding his eyes, his ears still ringing to the shots.

'F'Cris'sake, what they doin' out there?' croaked Sam.

Maloney did not dare to answer. Hank spat and kicked out again.

They finally cleared the scrub and headed for the cover of piled boulders at the foot of a rocky outcrop.

'Dismount,' said Maloney, reining to a halt. 'Hitch the mounts safe, and then we climb. There's a clear view of the trail from up there.'

It took no more than minutes for the three men to be within a few yards of the rim of the outcrop. The gunfire had ceased, the last shot whining to a high echo across the cloudless sky. A distressed horse snorted and stamped. Dust drifted in long slow slivers. An irate fly buzzed angrily.

'Easy does it,' murmured Maloney, gripping his drawn Colt as he drew himself the last three feet to the rim, lifted his head, stared at the trail below him, then slid back in a clatter of loose rocks and pebbles and vomited where he lay.

They mounted the rim of the outcrop slowly, silently save for the crunch and scramble of stones under boots, the hiss and heave of breath. Hank was the first to stand tall and take in the carnage of the scene below him.

'Ye gods of all hell,' he murmured as his gaze moved disbelievingly over the dead bodies of five of Casey's bar girls sprawled in the dirt like thrown aside trash.

'Goddamnit,' hissed Sam, coming to Hank's side, his face a streaming mass of dust and sweat.

Maloney holstered his Colt, wiped a hand across his mouth and spat violently across a rock. 'Massacre,' he croaked. 'A bloody massacre. Let's get down there.'

The girls' dresses had been torn from their bodies and left in the dirt like crushed blooms; one, a dusty shade of once bright blue, covered a girl's face as if placed there as a shroud to hide her staring eyes.

Sam moved round the wagon to the body of Myram Casey. 'Shot in the back,' he murmured.

Some distance away, a Winchester still clutched in his fingers, lay the twisted shape of Joe Burns. He had been knifed – the blade buried deep in his neck – then shot at close range through the head.

'They've taken Alice,' said Maloney, stepping between the bodies of the girls as he inspected each face, praying silently that one might flicker a hope of life. 'Alice ain't here.'

Hank kicked angrily at a rock. 'Still makin' sure they've got a hostage, ain't they? Still backin' all the odds. The filthy, murderin', sonsofbitches!' He drew his Colt as if to fire blindly at the nearest target facing him, thought better of it and holstered the weapon again with a defiant thud. 'I'm for fightin',' he announced.

'Ain't we all,' said Maloney turning from the carnage to narrow his gaze on the shimmering emptiness of the land. 'And mebbe that's just what they'd like us to do, unless they've ridden on to the border.'

'No chance,' said Sam. 'They're back in town waitin' on that showdown with Carew. You can bet to it.'

'And just where the hell was he when he was

needed?' sneered Hank, kicking another rock down the trail.

Maloney turned sharply. 'We need to get these bodies cleared. We've still got the wagon and team, so we'll drive 'em to the creek. Can't hide this from Doc and the townsfolk. Wouldn't be right. Let's get busy.'

'We goin' to fight?' persisted Hank, resting a hand on the butt of his Colt. 'We ain't goin' to just leave it, are we, do nothin'? Damnit, we can't walk away, pretend it never happened. We've got to fight, get back there to town, and fight.'

'And so we will,' said Sam. 'Ain't no man gets to see what we're seein' now and walks away. But blusterin' our way into town, guns all blazin', ain't goin' to achieve nothin', save add to the pile of bodies. And that ain't what these poor souls would want. T'ain't what they're goin' to get neither, not if I have my way. I say we talk to Doc and the others and decide some plan. Mebbe that'll include Carew; mebbe it won't. What do you reckon, Sheriff?'

Maloney cleared the sweat from his face and neck. 'You're right,' he said. 'We get to Bottom Creek soon as we can. Any luck we'll make it before nightfall.' He glanced quickly at Hank. 'Don't worry, we'll be fightin'. You'll see.'

But had Sheriff Maloney been honest with himself that afternoon, he had no idea how, when or where.

CHAPTER SEVENTEEN

Elmore Kelly strode the length of the early evening shadowed bar, his steps flat, heavy, measured, turned at the batwings and stared at the faces concentrated on him.

Bonehead purred like a self-satisfied cat after a kill at the shoulder of the captured bar girl. His brother Chad lounged, seemingly at quiet ease, at a table in a corner, his fingers working thoughtfully over the shape and feel of a newly opened bottle of whiskey. It would be another three minutes before he poured himself a measure. That was his way.

Elmore grunted and turned his gaze to the gang's three remaining sidekicks. They had said little since the frenzy of the killings at the wagon. Now, a bottle and three glasses placed on the table between them, they brooded like sullen owls, their eyes shifty and unable to focus on anything for more than a few hurried seconds. They murmured among themselves from time to time in anxious whispers hissed through clenched teeth. One going by the name of Jenks, drummed the fingers of his right hand on the stained tabletop, each lift and fall of a finger adding emphasis to his whispered words.

The scumbags were plotting something, thought Elmore, same as they always were, just like they had since hitting this godforsaken town. 'You got somethin' to say, then say it so's we can all hear,' he quipped, moving to the centre of the bar. 'Well?'

'We've been reckonin', boss,' said Jenks, coming carefully to his feet.

'Reckonin', eh?' mocked Kelly. 'That sounds mighty painful for types of your quality.'

The man disregarded the quip and stood his ground. 'What we did out there, shootin' up them women like we did, we ain't none of us done nothin' like that before, and we ain't much for it. We're kinda gettin' to think as how there'll be some awful retribution sought when them bodies are found. The sort of retribution handed out by Marshal Carew.' The man swallowed and began to sweat. 'If you get our meanin',' he added lamely.

Bonehead lost his concentration on the girl and spat across to the spittoon. 'We ain't back on that, are we?' he moaned. 'Hell, if they're for pullin' out, Elmore, let the rats go. I'm sick of 'em. Give 'em their shares and let's see the back of 'em.'

Chad Kelly finally poured himself a measure of whiskey and sank it in a single gulp. 'Agreed,' he said, replacing the glass. 'Let 'em go. If they're gettin' spooked with thoughts of retribution, then they ain't for the Kelly gang no more. Carew can have 'em – and I'm sure he will!'

Jenks swallowed again and blinked through his sweat. 'T'ain't like you're thinkin'. We ain't no cowards. Nossir. And we ain't for backin' out on you, that ain't to our reckonin'. It's just that—'

Elmore raised a commanding hand. 'Say no more, t'ain't necessary. Chad there will get your shares and you can ride. Right now. No messin'. You can leave the likes of Carew to us.' He grinned and let his eyes dance crazily in his head. 'But a word of warnin' to all three of you: if me or my brothers set so much as half an eye on you in the future, you're dead men. Dead, wherever you are, whatever the time of day or night. And that's a promise I look forward to keepin'.'

Jenks put a finger to his lips for silence as he led his two partners through one deep trough of shadow to the next, waited a moment, then settled to assess their chances of reaching the rear of the livery in one quick dash.

'What we waitin' for?' hissed the lean-faced fellow at Jenks's back. 'There ain't nobody about.'

'There don't *seem* to be nobody about,' returned Jenks, his eyes narrowing. 'Which ain't to say we got a clear run.'

'Longer we wait, worse it'll be,' murmured the third man, fingering his drawn Colt nervously. 'Let's get it over with. Once into the livery and saddled up there ain't nobody goin' to stop us.' He spat quietly into the dirt at his feet and tapped the lean-faced man on the shoulder with the barrel of his gun. 'You just hang on real safe to them bags of money you're carryin' there. I got plans for my split.'

'No worries,' quipped the man. 'We've all got plans, ain't we?'

'Cut the talk and concentrate,' snapped Jenks, irritably. 'Only plannin' we're doin' right now is figurin' on when to make a run for it.'

The three men fell into an uneasy silence, conscious now of the evening shadows thickening and the light in the far west slipping ever closer to the horizon.

'Be full dark in another hour,' hissed the man with the gun.

'Good,' murmured Jenks. 'We can sure as hell use it.'

They waited another full minute before easing like ponderous insects to the next depth of shadow. Another pause, more moments of waiting, watching, listening, then Jenks lifted his arm a fraction, glanced back at his companions, and broke cover in a sudden flurry of dust.

They went fast and low and hard for the livery, Jenks leading, a Winchester tight in his grip, the lean-faced man sweating under the weight of the three bags he carried, the third man craning his head to left and right for the slightest movement, the Colt gleaming on the streams of late light.

They skidded and tumbled into the gloom of the livery stabling and collapsed breathless against the piled mounds of straw and sacks of feed.

'Made it!' beamed lean-face throwing the bags to the floor. 'Now for the horses.'

'Not so fast,' said Jenks, gripping the Winchester in a fresh hold. 'This is all gettin' too easy.'

The man with the Colt eased to the side of the open door and peered over the ground they had just crossed. 'You're right,' he croaked. 'Too damned easy by half. How come Kelly let us go like he did? Last man to try that got a bullet for his trouble. How come Chad handed over the money so easy? T'ain't in his nature to be one spit co-operative. So what's the thinkin'? They plannin' on shootin' us on the way out?'

'Or figurin' on Carew doin' the job for 'em,' said Jenks, stepping to the other side of the door to scan the silent, empty street.

'We're bait,' said lean-face, plucking a strand of straw from his sweat-soaked stubble. 'Just bait. The Kelly boys are reckonin' on us flushin' out Carew for them. Hell!'

'Easy,' said Jenks, still watching the street. 'We ain't done yet. Get them horses back there saddled up. And stow them money bags, one to each mount. Minute they're ready, we hit the dirt hell-for-leather, headin' due north, away from the saloon. Once on the trail we ride hard for two miles, then turn to the scrub and rocks and let the night do the rest. First light and we'll be miles clear headin'—'

They heard the step, but did not see the man who made it. Not then.

Jenks took a grip of the lean-faced man's arm. 'Don't move,' he croaked. 'Not a muscle.' He screwed his eyes to peer into the thickening gloom. 'Who's there? Step forward whoever you are.' He gulped. The three men stared, watched and waited. A horse snorted, stamped a hoof. The silence settled like a blanket.

'Damn it, man, move!' hissed Jenks, releasing his grip on the lean-faced man's arm as he ranged the barrel of the Winchester from his hip. 'Don't think I won't use this, mister, 'cus I sure as hell will.'

'Do it, blast him now,' urged the third man, his face lathering in a cold, clinging sweat. He leaned forward, balanced on a step he dared not take. It's Carew,' he tremored. 'I can feel it's him.'

'Don't talk—' began Jenks, but too late in the suddenly shattered silence as the sidekick's gun roared in a blind, panicked aim.

Jenks fell back. The lean-faced man's gun roared in reaction to the first shot, the aim equally wild and blind.

'Sonofa—' spluttered Jenks, trying now to bring the Winchester into his full grip. He fell back again, lost his balance and crashed to the floor, his gaze widening in horror as he watched first the lean-faced man thrown back under the shattering blaze of twin Colts, then the third man spin like a top, showering a rain of blood, before sprawling lifeless in a spread of horse manure.

When the Colts roared again it was to silence a moaned plea for mercy that the man behind the guns chose not to hear.

CHAPTER EIGHTEEN

'They're buried, decent as we can make it in the circumstances. At least they ain't been left to the buzzards.' Doc Parker gazed sorrowfully round the gathering of townsmen and women assembled by the wagons in the soft evening light, and mopped his wet brow carefully. 'Worse thing I've ever seen, and I guess I speak for the rest of you.'

'Too right,' murmured a man, comforting his tearful wife. 'Devils who did that should be strung up.'

'Hangin's too good for 'em,' echoed another.

The gathering fell back to a stunned quiet in which only whispers could be heard as folk consoled their loved ones, friends and neighbours, stifled their anger and closed their eyes if not their minds to the horrors of the scenes they had witnessed as Sam Carr, Sheriff Maloney and Hank Forman had brought the wagon containing the bodies of the girls, Casey and Joe Burns into the shelter of Bottom Creek, and the silent burial that had accompanied Doc's words of committal. Now, they could only stand, talking quietly among themselves, and try to ponder all that had happened during the past few days.

'We could have an ugly mob intent on blood when this finally sinks in,' said Doc, drawing Sam and the sheriff aside to the shadow of a wagon. 'We need to have a plan. Any ideas?'

'The Kellys are still holdin' the town, and Alice,' murmured Maloney. 'A frenzied all-out attack will fill Boot Hill twice over. I ain't for that.'

'Me neither,' agreed Doc. 'But you can see the mood that's beginnin' to brew. Give it another hour, and I won't be able to control 'em. They'll be wantin' revenge, any way, at any price.' He cleared the sticky night sweat from his neck. 'Any sign of Carew?'

'None,' grunted Sam.

'Any hope of makin' contact.'

'Not unless we scour the town room by room; every nook and cranny,' said Maloney, leaning back on the wagon. 'And while we're doin' that, Kellys could be pickin' us off like frogs in a pail.'

'Mebbe that's worth a try,' persisted Doc. 'Hell, it's about all we got.'

'That's about it, Doc – all we got,' muttered Sam. He stared hard at Maloney. 'Goin' to have to go back, aren't we? No choice. Go back and get to Carew before he either pulls out or the folk here hit town for a blood bath.'

Maloney pushed himself clear of the wagon. 'Can you handle things here, Doc?' he asked. 'T'ain't goin' to be easy.'

'I can if I have the time,' said Doc. 'I've got to

start reasonin' with 'em.' He paused for a moment. 'Here's how I'll do it: I'll explain you've gone back to town to establish contact with Carew. You take Hank with you. When you've done whatever you can, Hank will ride back here, tell us what's happenin', and we'll then bring a force of every able-bodied man to the edge of town soon after sun-up tomorrow. Best I can offer right now.'

'That'll do,' said Maloney. 'Meantime, we'll freshen up, get somethin' to eat, then ride.'

'Do me a favour, will you, Doc,' murmured Sam. 'Look to that boy of mine, will you? He's with the Matthews' outfit right now, but I'd sure be grateful for you keepin' an eye to him.'

'Leave it to me,' said Doc. 'As for you—'

'Don't say it, Doc,' clipped Maloney, slapping Doc's shoulder. 'Just pray.'

'The money. What about the money? Was it there?' Elmore Kelly's eyes burned with a gleam so intense that they seemed to pierce the dimly lit saloon bar at the Palace like beams; nor did he blink, not once, or so much as flicker his lids as he watched his brother's face and waited for him to speak. 'Well?' he added, the word creaking into the silence like a step across a loose board.

'Gone. Weren't there. Not a cent of it.' Bone-head swallowed and adjusted the set of his pants. 'And don't think I didn't look. I did. Turned that damned livery over. Every corner. Every muck heap. It weren't there. Simple as that.'

'Three dead bodies, but no money,' murmured

Chad. 'Strange, unless they hid it before they got themselves killed.' He smiled and strolled across the bar to the batwings and stared into the deepening night. 'Or unless Carew took it.'

' 'Course he took it,' snapped Elmore. 'Who else? He shot them yellow-bellied scum and helped himself. He's countin' it somewhere out there right now. The rat!' He spat into the spittoon and paced into the shadows.

'That's it then, ain't it?' said Bonehead, searching out a fresh bottle of whiskey at the back of the bar. 'We cut our losses right here, take the girl and pull out tonight. What do you reckon, Chad?'

'Mebbe,' said his brother, his gaze narrowed on the dark street. 'Mebbe not.'

'No question to it to my reckonin'.' Bonehead opened the bottle and slopped a measure to a stained glass. 'Hell, we're down to the three of us, and it's only a matter of time before them townsfolk find them girls out there on the trail – then they'll come ridin' like fire on the wind. Three guns and a girl hostage ain't goin' to be no use in that heat. But if we leave now. . . .'

'Not while Carew's still standin',' growled Elmore, emerging from the shadows to the glow of the single lamp.

'Damn Carew,' gestured Bonehead. 'To hell with him. Ain't he done enough? You want to give him the satisfaction of goin' on, pinnin' us down here, watchin' and waitin' on every breath, spookin' ourselves to the bone? We've got the girl here, let's use her. Damn it, we can always kill her later when we're all through.' He grinned at Alice tied to a chair at a nearby table. 'Don't worry, lady, I'll make it quick.'

Alice shivered and stared through wild, white eyes.

Chad Kelly turned from the batwings and stood with his back to the night. 'We ain't never been split in our doin' and thinkin', not since Ma died and we rode free. Always the three of us. Always together. One don't break to leave the others. Two don't split to abandon one. We're the Kelly brothers. Don't let's forget that.'

Elmore grunted and twitched his shoulders. 'He's right. That's the way of it.'

'So I ain't for not bein' together, just like you say,' smiled Bonehead. 'You bet to it. Always have been. Ain't that what we promised Ma when she lay dyin'? Didn't we promise as how we'd each look to the other? Hell, I ain't forgotten that, and I ain't for breakin' the promise, but even so—'

'Why don't you rest up some, little Brother?' said Elmore, his gaze softening. 'Take it easy for an hour or so. Me and Chad here can do the watchin' and waitin'. Ain't much goin' to happen tonight. Come first spit of light and we'll all be agreed, the three of us, on what's to be done. So you just take that little girl there and go enjoy yourself 'til we call you. You've earned it. But you save some for us, eh? You just do that.' He stared directly into Bonehead's eyes. 'Do it, little Brother. Now.'

115

*

Alice sat on the edge of the bed and waited for Bonehead to lock the door and close on her like a vulture. She would not fight; she was too exhausted, mentally and physically. There were too many images tumbling hopelessly, wildly through her head, too many memories jostling and clawing like frantic bodies. She was for giving in now. The strength to fight had been sapped.

She swallowed and watched carefully, without seeming to breathe, as Bonehead crossed the room to the darkened window and peered into the night-shadowed street. His gaze, narrowed and tight, moved to the left, then to the right, to the left again; monotonously, mechanically like a beam.

'Don't you move none, gal,' he murmured, without looking at Alice. 'You just sit there and stay real quiet. Bonehead ain't for harmin' you none, you rest assured to that.'

Alice swallowed again, felt her fingers tightening on the spread to the unmade bed. Last time a man had made a promise like that, he had half killed her.

'There's other matters need tendin',' Bonehead continued, still peering from the window. 'You bet. And I ain't fooled none. Nossir. They don't fool Bonehead that easy.' He mumbled a throaty growl to his thoughts. 'You hearin' me, gal?'

'I'm listenin',' said Alice, stifling a sudden shudder. 'What – what you lookin' for?'

'Him,' snapped Bonehead. 'That louse Carew who's been like a tick in my shirt for months. He's there, some place. I got the measure of him, even though them brothers of mine don't rate me none.' He turned a sweat-streaked face to Alice. 'Been here before, ain't you? That room next door, weren't that where Carew took out one of my partners and grabbed you?' Alice nodded. 'Figured so. Well, it ain't goin' to happen a second time. No chance.'

'What do you mean?' croaked Alice, twitching at the shaft of another shudder.

Bonehead scanned the street again. 'Hell, them two down there in the bar must reckon me for bein' some mule . . . *Go take it easy, Bonehead, go enjoy yourself with the girl* . . . That's just so much whiskey-talk. They want me out of the way so's they can start cuttin' the money fifty-fifty. And you know what, they figure for Carew somehow gettin' to us and finishin' me. Oh, yes, gal, that's their thinkin' plain enough. Seen 'em plot like that before. You bet. But, hell, I'm their own flesh and blood, f'Cris'sake. Their own brother.' He wiped a hand over his wet face. 'And it's all because of Carew. All down to him. Well, he ain't havin' me. Not no how, he ain't.'

Alice stood up slowly, her legs weak and trembling, her body suddenly chilled as if about to crack. She stepped softly to the far side of the window and pressed her back to the wall. 'You plannin' on pullin' out?' she asked. 'Ridin' clear?'

'I'm plannin' on *us* pullin' out, lady – you and me, together. And you're goin' to guarantee that for the both of us, on your life. So get thinkin', fast. How we goin' to get out of here without Carew knowin' to it?'

CHAPTER NINETEEN

There was a way, the only way. The same escape route she and Carew had used. But would it serve again; would a flight to the rear of the Palace through the door in the corridor to the outside stairway go undetected a second time? Suppose Carew was waiting. Would Bonehead shoot her first then face the marshal? She might get killed in the crossfire, anyhow. Or might the Kellys be there, as silent as waiting ghosts?

Alice stiffened her back against the wall and glanced at Bonehead as he continued to scan the inky black street as if expecting the shadows to leap into sudden life. He was not fooling. He firmly believed his brothers to be in the process of double-crossing him and hoping for his death at the hands of Carew. So much for the bonds of blood!

She turned her gaze to the room again and closed her eyes, her thoughts spinning crazily from the wagon, the girls, to the gunfire, the slaughter and mayhem all around her; then to Doc Parker, the sheriff, Sam Carr, the townsfolk, the darkness of the street that seemed somehow to mirror the despair and emptiness of the future. There would be no future. . . .

'We ain't got all night, lady,' hissed Bonehead.

Alice opened her eyes, cleared her head and pushed herself away from the wall. 'There's a door to the back,' she said, tossing her hair to her neck. 'Far end of the corridor. It isn't locked. Steps there drop to the storehouses and outbuildings.' She flashed a glance. 'It's the only way.'

'Then we'll take it,' said Bonehead, deserting the window for the door. 'Shift.'

They crept slowly from the room, leaving the door ajar behind them, and went like night cats along the corridor above the bar to the door at the far end. Here, Bonehead gestured for Alice to open it. 'Not a sound,' he hissed, pausing a moment to catch any movement or voices in the saloon. Nothing. He nodded, and Alice eased the door open to the softest of creaks on the tired hinges.

They waited. The balmy night lathered their already wet faces. Alice peered fearfully through the gap to the stairway. There were no shapes she could recognize in the smothering darkness; no sounds, no movements, only the palest of glows at the Palace batwings from the trimmed lamp in the bar.

Bonehead gestured again to move on, prodding Alice to the stairway, then creeping silently in her steps. They were halfway down, the tumble of sheds and outbuildings taking on a darker bulk in the blackness, when Alice stopped, stared down to the cluttered ground below her and hissed for Bonehead to stop.

'You hear somethin', gal?' he muttered on a tight, strained breath. 'Don't you fool with me none. I ain't in no mood for it.'

'Thought I did,' hissed Alice, wiping a twist of sweat from her chin. 'Must've been mistaken.'

'Move on,' ordered Bonehead.

They reached the ground and ducked quickly into the cover of the nearest outbuilding and its jumble of boxes, crates and empty barrels.

'Good,' grinned Bonehead, his gleaming face awash with sweat. 'Now for the horses.'

'Where are they?'

'Hitched in an open barn just short of the livery.'

Alice swallowed. 'That means crossing open ground.'

'That means *you* crossin' open ground. You're goin' to fetch 'em. Move!'

They slid on from the cover, the darkness seeming now to clamour round them as if resenting a disturbing presence, Alice's mind whirling once again with images and jumbled thoughts. Crossing the open ground to the old barn would be almost easy by comparison with what she had faced so far. But what then; what to do once she was in the barn?

She could do nothing, stay right there, not move and wait for Carew to find Bonehead. She could make a run for it, try to get clear, lose herself in the night. But Bonehead Kelly was a deal smarter than to let her do that. And what would happen when he had his horse all saddled up and ready to ride? Would he continue to hold her hostage against getting safely clear, or would he simply kill her where she stood? Dying where she stood might be a better option.

'Wait.' Bonehead clamped a hand on Alice's arm as they reached a line of broken fencing fronting the open ground. They squatted, waited, watched. Bonehead wiped the sweat from his neck. 'This ain't a safe place,' he muttered. 'Too open. No cover.' His eyes narrowed. 'We cross together.'

Alice bit her lip. 'And then?'

Bonehead's wet, gleaming face creased into a long grin. 'Then we ride together. You're comin' with me.'

The old barn seemed deeper, darker than the night itself, thought Alice, as she watched Bonehead set about saddling two horses.

They had crossed the open ground quickly, silently, their bodies bent, their steps moving safely through the soft sand and scattered tufts of growth. Alice's eyes had darted to left and right, hoping, praying for a sight of something that might hint of Carew's presence. But the darkness stayed silent, empty, broken only by the moonlight, the single glow of the lamp at the saloon. Nothing had moved save their shadows as they finally made it to the barn and disappeared inside.

Alice stifled a shudder, flicked her hair into her

neck and folded her arms across her breasts. The stance might look defiant, might even fool Bonehead for a moment, but deep in her gut she was uncertain, confused and scared. Bonehead would make her ride with him, and she would have no choice and no strength to resist. And death, she figured, would not come until she had outlived her value as a hostage, something to be traded against whatever difficulty Bonehead encountered.

Where would he head, how long would she be riding? Who would ever come to know where she was, or where her life had ended?

'What about the money?' she croaked. 'You leavin' without it?'

'Forget it for now,' muttered Bonehead, continuing to work on the horses. 'I ain't fussed. I know where them scumbag brothers of mine'll be holin' up when they've done with Carew. And I'll be waitin' on takin' their shares. You bet I will!' He tightened a girth and stood back. 'You ride tight alongside me, you hear, real close. No gettin' ahead, no hangin' back. First time I see you pullin' clear, you're dead.'

Alice stifled another shudder, unfolded her arms and stepped towards the saddled horse. 'What about Carew?' she asked.

'If Carew's that close, he would have shown by now. Mebbe we got lucky. What the hell! Carew don't fret me none. Now you just mount up here, and then we're gone.'

'You hear that?' said Chad Kelly, positioning

123

himself at the side of the batwings and nodding to the night beyond them. 'Horses. That'll be our boneheaded brother scootin' out of town with the girl – and not a dollar to call his own.' He grinned and spat over the 'wings to the boardwalk. 'Darn fool.'

Elmore grunted as he continued to pack the stolen money into saddle-bags, his shadow bent like a feeding crow through the pale lamplight. 'Didn't expect any other, did you? Minute he got clear to that room, he started plannin'. Just like I knew he would, the fool. How far do you reckon he'll get?'

'Short odds on under a mile; a half if he's lucky. And then Carew will be waitin'. It's his style.' Chad listened to the fading beat of the hoofs. 'Always figured it might come to this,' he said thoughtfully. 'What is it with that brother of ours?'

'Same as it's always been – plain mule-headed. He don't never see more than what's in front of him, and when it don't suit, he rides.' Kelly's fingers worked quickly, silently through the piled money on the table in front of him. 'It's his choice, his fate. I ain't fussed none.'

'He's still kin,' said Chad, lighting a thin cheroot. 'Still blood.'

'What you sayin'? You reckonin' as how we should ride after him, save him from himself and Carew? You can. I ain't doin' no such thing. The money here will be ready and we'll be set minute Carew rides back into town. And then, Brother, we shall have the satisfaction of seekin' just and due revenge on the man who killed one of our own flesh and blood.' Elmore's eyes gleamed through the shadows like coals. 'Odd, ain't it, how things work out? Few days back we were the Kelly gang ridin' out where we chose. Now, we're two brothers of three. The last of the gang. Like I say, odd.'

Chad Kelly did not answer.

CHAPTER TWENTY

Alice felt her hair flying on the night breeze, the smooth caress of it across her face and shoulders, and flexed her fingers through the reins as her mount closed once again on Bonehead Kelly's horse.

The brooding silent bulks of Firebow were already behind them, the trail ahead like a grey skin where it wound its way through outcrops of rocks, scatterings of tight scrub and brush and the gentler slopes to the distant bluffs, now no more than vague areas of darkness.

Did Bonehead know where he was heading, had he a plan to a final destination, or was he just riding wild and blind, grateful to be clear of the town and the threat of the stalking Marshal Carew? But what of his brothers, wondered Alice, would they simply let him go, grateful in their own turn for finding themselves without the need to share the spoils of the Murchison raid? Would Elmore Kelly continue to wait for a showdown with Carew, or would they abandon Firebow and ride for the southern borders? Alice tensed in the sudden chill of a shiver as her thoughts spun crazily into images of the dead bodies of the bar girls, Myram Casey and Joe Burns, the leering pleasure of the Kelly boys at the massacre; and then the endless questions: where were Sheriff Maloney, Sam Carr, Doc Parker, Hank? What had happened to the townsfolk? Where. . . .

There was a shape, darker and denser than the night itself almost before she knew it. A rider up ahead, his mount silent and still at the foot of a sprawl of rocks where they spilled across the trail, his body straight and tensed.

Alice saw the gleam of a rifle barrel, the darting glint as it was levelled to its aim, heard the snort of Bonehead's mount under the sudden drag of reins, and sensed her own horse's growing confusion.

'In the name of all-hell!' roared Bonehead, above the thudding of hoofs, but the words hung uselessly in his throat and were lost in the clamour of snorts and whinnying, creaking leather and jangling tack, and the scattering of loose rocks and stones as the horses came to a sweat-soaked halt.

'Carew, damn his eyes!' groaned Bonehead.

Alice shivered, clutched at the reins to bring her mount under control, not daring to take her eyes off the rider ahead of them. Would he let loose a blaze of lead, take Bonehead captive and hand him over to Sheriff Maloney? There had been no doubting his intentions this far.

Now he simply sat, silent and motionless, the Winchester levelled, his gaze flat and steady, his shape silhouetted against the night sky's flitting moonlight.

'Stand aside, Marshal,' croaked Bonehead, both hands still tight on the reins. 'I ain't for pickin' no fight with you. I'm pullin' out. Ridin' on. You won't see no more of me. And I ain't takin' my share of any money. It's all back there.'

Alice shivered again, blinked and swallowed. Should she whip up her mount now and make a dash for it; ride anywhere, in any direction, just let the darkness take her and swallow her? She glanced quickly at Bonehead. Did he really think that a lawman was going to let him simply ride on, no more said, the blood of Murchison, the station, the massacre of the girls still dripping in his wake? If he did—

'Ride on, miss,' called Carew at last. 'Head east for the creek. The townsfolk'll be waitin'. There ain't nothin' for you here.'

Alice tensed, a trickle of cold sweat icing her spine. Bonehead made a half gesture with his right hand to his holstered Colt, saw the glint of the rifle barrel as it shifted to follow, and flexed his fingers to a tighter grip on the reins. He scowled at Alice. 'Do like he says,' he hissed, spitting into the dirt.

Alice reined her mount clear of the trail, paused a moment to stare at Carew, a dozen questions clambering through her mind, and eased to the scrub where the night seemed to hang like a shroud. Seconds later, she was gone, her horse pounding smoothly through the scrub and brush.

It was not until she had ridden for some

minutes, her mount picking its way at will on a loose rein, that the growth thinned again to sprawls of sand, stones and grit and she saw the vague line of a minor trail threading its way east. Then too, her eyes blurring, she heard the sharp crack and echoing whine through the night of two shots.

Rifle shots.

'How much longer?' Chad Kelly paced carefully across the floor at the batwings, glancing only briefly into the night-filled street where nothing came or went or moved.

'You ain't gettin' impatient, are you, Brother?' grinned Elmore, scratching his balding head before replacing his hat. 'T'ain't like you. You were always the easy-goin' one, full of patience, same as Ma. So what's eatin' you?'

Chad turned and paced back to the 'wings. 'Ain't nothin' eatin' me, nothin' of note anyhow, save this graveyard of a town. Takes some strange folk to just pull out like they did. They still out there at that creek? Why? What they doin', plannin' some sort of attack on us? Sittin' out there right now, or ridin' hard full of seethin' anger and revenge for the death of them girls? That it? Is that what's happenin'?'

Elmore stared hard at his brother for a long, silent moment when nothing seemed to fill the saloon bar save the ticking of the clock. He poured a slow measure of whiskey to a glass of already sticky dregs and turned it through his grubby fingers. 'This ain't Chad Kelly I'm hearin', is it, one of the fastest guns known through the territory, a feared and hated gunslinger? The same Chad Kelly who was two-parts of the mastermind behind the Murchison raid? Is this that same Chad Kelly?' He downed the drink in one gulp. 'I tell you, Brother, you ain't yourself. You sickenin' for somethin'?'

Chad turned back to the batwings and stared into the street. 'What got into Bonehead for him to go off like that? He ain't never done nothin' like that before?'

'Bonehead was gettin'—' began Elmore.

'I'll tell you what got to eatin' him: this town, this bar, that damned street out there. The whole stinkin' place! That's what got to him, same as it'll get to us if we don't do somethin' about it.' He turned slowly, his gaze dark, his face gleaming under a lathering of sweat. 'Or if Carew don't get to us first.'

'Carew again!' growled Elmore, pushing back his chair, stamping angrily to his feet. 'It always comes back to Carew.' He slopped another measure of whiskey to the glass and sank it behind a wincing gulp. 'Right. You bet. If that's it, if that's what's churnin' you up, we do somethin' about it. Now. This very minute. Before sun-up. We get out there and we find that sonofabitch. We put an end to him like we should've done long back. Agreed? You go along with that? Finish Carew here and then get clear with that money and go buy ourselves a long and comfortable life some place

130

south. What you say?'

'I say fine, just fine, Brother,' said Chad, his back to the 'wings. 'But before we do that, I suggest you take a look over my shoulder here and tell me what you see. . . .'

'Did they see you?' hissed Sam Carr, pressing himself tighter to the clapboard side of the mercantile as if wishing he could pass through it.

'Mebbe,' murmured Maloney at his side. 'One of them was at the 'wings. Chad, I think.' He swallowed and glanced quickly to left and right. 'Ain't nobody there now. We goin' on?'

'Got to. No choice,' said Sam. 'We heard them two shots out there as we came down the track, but who fired them? Carew? One of the Kellys? And why?' He too swallowed and licked at the cold sweat on his lips. 'Where's Alice, damn it?' He wiped his face. 'Best push on, make it to the back of the saloon, take stock from there. Meantime, keep watch for Carew. Got to be here, somewhere, ain't he?'

Maloney's gaze narrowed on the night. 'Unless. . . .' he began, but thought better of it at the sound of a creak from the batwings. 'Hell, somebody's movin'.'

'Who?'

'Elmore Kelly.'

'He alone?'

'So far.' Maloney's fingers tightened on his drawn Colt. 'Don't move.'

'You bet,' gulped Sam.

They sank deeper into the shadows until the clapboard joints were biting into their flesh like teeth, and watched wide-eyed and without blinking, as Elmore Kelly eased carefully along the shaded boardwalk fronting the saloon. They saw the flash of his eyes, the lines of concentration across his face, held their breath as it seemed for a moment that he looked directly at them from across the street.

Maloney toyed with the idea of risking a shot. Who knows, maybe he would get lucky. 'Don't even think it,' murmured Sam, as if reading his thoughts. Maloney flexed his fingers and continued to watch.

Kelly had turned somewhere deep in the shadows beyond the glow of the light from the bar, but made no move to return to the 'wings.

'What's happenin'?' hissed Sam, the sweat coursing down his cheeks.

'I don't get it. He ain't movin'. Just watchin'.'

A curl of cigar smoke drifted into the street like a furl of breath. A board creaked. A step sounded. More smoke. Another creak.

'He's movin' again,' croaked Maloney.

Sam gulped.

'Now just who the hell is it out there?' called Kelly, across the darkness, his voice seeming to seep through the boardwalk. 'T'ain't you, is it, Marshal? No, I reckon not. So who we got for company this night? You one of them townsfolk? Mebbe it's the sheriff himself, eh? The lawman come to bring the Kelly gang to book. That it?

Well, let me tell you somethin', fella, lawmen don't fuss us none. Nossir. We usually end up killin' 'em.'

Cigar smoke curled again. The night air grew thicker, tighter. Maloney shifted uneasily. Sam Carr held his breath and sweated.

'You hearin' me, fella?' came the voice again. ' 'Course you are. You're there, watchin', ain't you? Well, now, let's see what you're really made of, eh? You care to step out and show yourself, or do I have to come across there myself?'

CHAPTER
TWENTY-ONE

'Don't get to bein' no hero,' urged Sam, laying a hand on Maloney's arm. 'That rat can't be trusted.'

'I know,' murmured the sheriff. 'But just what in hell's name is he playin' at?'

'Whatever, it ain't healthy.'

Maloney's fingers danced across the butt of his Colt. His eyes narrowed as if to pierce the shadows on the boardwalk. He glanced quickly at the faint glow in the bar. 'Mebbe you'd best make a move, Sam,' he croaked. 'Slip away somehow. I figure for Kelly reckonin' on there bein' only me out here. He ain't seen you yet.'

'Can't leave you now,' said Sam, clearing the sweat again. 'Hell, supposin'—'

'Do it, Sam. There ain't no point in both of us puttin' ourselves in Kelly's sights. Get away. Anywhere. Find Carew and Alice.' He flashed a tight piercing gaze. 'Do it, f'Cris'sake!'

Sam wiped at the sweat again, nodded and switched his concentration from the empty street to the darkness around him. Left or right? Back towards the deserted saddlery, or on beyond the mercantile to Walt Sweeney's timber store and yard? Once there, he could maybe lose himself among the wood piles and crates.

He decided on the timber yard and slid away without another word.

'What you doin', fella?' Kelly's voice growled across the shadow-thick street as if echoing from a deep pit somewhere in it. 'You ain't gettin' jelly-legged now, are you? Hell, mister, you've come this far; ain't no point in delayin' it, is there? Step clear and let's be doin' this.'

But was there an edge of impatience in Kelly's voice, wondered Sam, pausing to catch his breath behind a split barrel? Was he getting tired of waiting for Maloney to show his face; fearful perhaps that Carew might put in an appearance? And where were his brothers? Maloney had seen Chad at the batwings, but what of Bonehead, had he been out there on the trail? And where was Alice?

Sam scurried on like a beetle to the timber yard and slid behind a pile of rough hewn planks, his eyes narrowing to concentrate on what he could see of the street. Nothing of Kelly save the drifting curl of cigar smoke growing thinner by the minute, and no movement from Maloney still hugging the shadows on the boardwalk at the mercantile.

Somebody was going to have to move, damn it!

He winced at the cramp in his aching limbs,

shifted his position and let his gaze wander to the glow of light from the bar. No sign there of any comings and goings, so what if. . . ? It was then that Sam's gaze had lifted to the spread of dark windows on the first floor. Had he seen a movement at the window on the far left? A person, a trick of the pale moonlight? Or perhaps a sniping gun, waiting to pick off Maloney the second he stepped into the street. Hell, the sheriff would be gunned down like a dog!

Sam had made to move, get back to the mercantile and warn Maloney of the danger, when the sheriff stepped from the shadows to the edge of the boardwalk.

'Oh, no,' murmured Sam under his breath. 'Don't—'

The glowing butt of the discarded cigar had reached the street ahead of Elmore Kelly's looming bulk. He paused, eyed Maloney like a hawk spotting its prey, and grinned.

'Lawman,' he sneered. 'I might have known. Don't never give up, do you?' He took a slow step over the parched dirt. 'Another lawman. . . .'

Sam gulped, croaked a curse that never made it across his lips, blinked on a wash of sweat and began slowly, almost painfully, to come upright behind the timbers.

Maloney had taken another step, left the boardwalk, reached the dirt.

'Fool!' hissed Sam. 'Don't—'

The roar of the Winchester from the saloon's first-floor window shattered the night silence to splintered echoes.

Elmore Kelly stood his ground without moving a muscle or flexing so much as a finger across his holstered Colt, his gaze still hawkish as Maloney spun, clawed for his gun, rolled back and was tossed like a broken leaf to the ground on the blaze of the sniper's second shot.

Sam sank behind the wood pile in a lathering of sweat and shivered uncontrollably.

It was a full five, agonizing minutes before Sam dared to move again; before his head stopped spinning, the images flashing and fading like flame, and the sounds finally drifted beyond the silence of the empty night. He could smell the cordite from the gunshots, the very blood and sweat that had dripped to the dirt and lay now beneath the crumpled body of Sheriff Maloney.

Sam swallowed on his parched throat, blinked and cleared the cold sweat from his face. He eased his stiff, aching limbs from what seemed to be the teeth of a trap behind the pile of planks, and hoisted himself high enough to peer into the street again.

All quiet now, nothing moving, no sounds, only the shadows standing like mourners around the sheriff's body. Sam's fingers dug into the timber as a sudden surge of anger welled within him.

'Sonofa-goddamn-bitch,' he cursed quietly. 'Damned if I don't just get myself—' And he then brought himself up sharply. Nothing to be gained by adding to the body count, save to give them

Kelly boys the satisfaction of watching another man squirm to his death. If he took so much as a step through the batwings. . . . 'Forget it,' he muttered.

He shifted his gaze to the deserted buildings, the deep trenches of darkness, the looming, sometimes leering shadows that seemed to mock. 'Get to Carew,' he muttered again. 'Or mebbe wait for Doc and the townsmen. . . .' His fingers drummed lightly on the timbers. He frowned. One thing was for certain, he pondered, the Kellys had obviously reckoned for Maloney being alone. And that gave Sam Carr an edge.

Time to use it.

Elmore Kelly scooped the last of the money from the table to an already bulging saddle-bag, fastened it with a grunted tug and stood back with an air or satisfaction.

'A whole sight more than we'd reckoned on, Brother,' he muttered, filling a waiting glass with whiskey. 'Yessir, one helluva sight more now that we ain't for splittin' a dozen ways. Damnit, we could near buy ourselves a town, let alone a prairie stake some place.'

He tossed the drink to the back of his throat and smacked his lips. 'Mebbe we'll do just that, eh? Find ourselves a town down south and buy it, just like that, lock, stock and barrel. What you say, Brother?'

'I'm askin' myself if that dead lawman out there came alone,' said Chad, pacing slowly from a window to the batwings, his gaze dark and concentrated. 'Town sheriff don't normally work without a sidekick, 'specially when he's lost his town.'

Elmore poured another drink and lit a cigar. 'You're a frettin' man and no mistake, Brother,' he grinned behind a veil of smoke. 'Who in hell cares right now? He's dead, we're here, set to pull out, and it's my bettin' that scumbag Carew is still sweatin' over Bonehead and that two-bit bar-room whore. So why we worryin', Brother, tell me that?'

' 'Cus it don't feel right, that's why,' snapped Chad, watching the street as if waiting for it to fill with a sudden light.

Elmore sneered and blew a thick stream of smoke. ' 'Cus it don't feel right – well, it didn't feel right, I'll remind you, the day we hit the bank at Pondsville, and it sure as hell didn't *feel right* by your reckonin' when we held up the stage out of Red Forks, not to mention the rail job out Menire way. And who was it havin' second thoughts at Greenstown? It was you, Chad, you and only you. Now, I'm all for caution and thinkin' things through, that way we stay alive, but sometimes you can get to seein' a whole heap of trouble where it don't exist.'

'We almost fouled up at Greenstown,' reflected Chad.

'Almost, but not quite. Like now: we've lost men, lost Brother Bonehead, but we ain't lost the money and we're within a spit of an open trail to most anywhere of our choosin'. So let's ride, eh, let's put this town behind us same as we've done a dozen times before.'

But Elmore Kelly's words were already fading on the night as Chad stepped through the batwings and let them creak closed behind him. He stared in chilled silence at the sight approaching him.

CHAPTER
TWENTY-TWO

Bonehead Kelly's body had been roped into the saddle of his mount, two hewn branches keeping him upright, his feet lashed into the stirrups, his arms stiff as poles at his side so that his head was thrust back to leave his wide, blind eyes staring like dead moons into the night sky. The words, CAREW IS COMING, had been scrawled across a board and hung round his neck.

'In the name of hell. . . .' murmured Chad, as the horse made its slow, scuffing way down the street. A beading of sweat broke like rain across his brow and dripped in cold splashes to his cheeks.

'My God,' croaked Elmore, stepping into the street, his cigar dusting ash across the dirt, the smoke spiralling to the shadows.

They stood in silence until the mount drew level with the glow from the saloon bar and stopped as if knowing instinctively that its journey was done.

'That no-good sonofabitch marshal. . . .' hissed Elmore, the colour rising through his cheeks and into the very roots of his eyeballs. 'I should've done for that louse long back . . . I should have, damnit!'

'This ain't the time for should haves,' ordered Chad, reaching for the reins to the mount. 'This is time for shiftin'. Get this sight off the street. I'll go get our horses, then we're ridin' out of this hell-hole.'

'You see them words writ there,' said Elmore, staring at the scrawled message on the board at Bonehead's neck. 'See what they say?'

'I can read, Brother,' mouthed Chad, 'but I ain't payin' no heed. I say we ride now, and that's just what we're goin' to do.' He turned abruptly on his heel, drew his Colt and headed into the shadows for the livery.

Sam Carr calmed a sudden shiver across his shoulders and melted silently into the deeper darkness at the side of a ramshackle lean-to. He blinked, closed his eyes for a moment and was back in an instant to the sight of Bonehead Kelly roped to his horse. The gunslinger's death must have been from the shots he and the sheriff had heard earlier; Carew had tracked him, killed him, freed Alice perhaps. And now . . . Where was he now? Waiting in any one of the shadows? Stalking, aware, watching. A killer loose in the night.

Sam shook his head clear of the images and questions. Concentrate, he told himself, think this through, where you are, what has happened, what to do next.

The sheriff was dead; Bonehead had fallen to Carew; that left Elmore and Chad still breathing. Chad was out here somewhere, heading for the old barn at the side of the livery, doubtless to collect mounts and saddle up for a fast ride out of town before first light. Was Elmore going to forget his showdown with Carew? Did the Murchison bank haul mean more? Chad would have had something to say on that score.

Sam took in his surroundings. Rubbish, old timbers, crates, barrels, a broken wheel. He would push on, he decided. Make for the livery. Maybe Carew had holed up there. Or maybe he could disturb Chad, take him by surprise. Maybe.

He slid away.

Somewhere in Sam's mind a clock was ticking. He was conscious of the night's deeper darkness ebbing away, of a first smudge of a new day's light already spreading across the eastern skies. The shadows looked suddenly awake and stretching.

He had reached the broken fence of the small corral that backed on to the barn at the side of the livery and paused to catch his breath, figure his next move and wonder if there was the slightest chance of Doc and the townsmen reaching the outskirts of town. He was confident they would not approach closer until full light. But if Elmore Kelly and his brother succeeded in saddling up and riding out on the main trail, there was a fair chance. . . .

A horse snorted, another stamped. Sam stiff-

143

ened. Chad Kelly was in the barn. 'Hell,' he cursed on a soft breath, as he crouched low and made for the end of the fencing. There was a side door that always stood open on rusted hinges. Maybe he could sneak through it, spook Kelly sufficient to hold him up until either he or Carew. . . .

A horse snorted again. There was a jangle of tack, the creak of leather. A slow, easy voice soothed and assured. Sam licked his lips, wiped his hands down his pants, then spat into the palms and rubbed them together.

'Here goes, Sam Carr!' he told himself, and crossed to the barn in a dozen rapid strides.

Too late. He was about to squeeze through the open door, when Chad Kelly, mounted and trailing a second horse roped behind him, emerged from the barn and reined round to head to the saloon.

He saw Sam in an instant and flashed his Colt in a lightning draw at the same time as he reined the mount back and steadied it where it stood.

'Stand back there, fella,' snapped Kelly, the Colt's barrel gleaming in a sudden shaft of light. 'I ain't for no more killin' in this hell-hole town, but I ain't for wastin' good time neither. So either get out of my sights or—'

The crash of collapsing timber behind Kelly froze Sam to the spot. A stack of logs used by Sam for fuelling the forge, had somehow been disturbed by someone to set the heftiest of the logs spinning down the slight slope to the barn.

'Carew?' murmured Sam, backing to the barn wall as Kelly's mount reared, wild-eyed and frenzied. Kelly cursed, clung desperately with one hand to the reins while the other continued to threaten uselessly with the Colt.

Kelly made one last bid to control the mount, but without a hope under the trundling spread of logs and momentum in their dash down the slope.

Sam turned, panic-stricken now, to the open door, gripped the edge of it, but was toppled as a log spun across his heels. He heard Kelly curse again and watched, sweat-soaked and breathless as the gunslinger hit the dirt to add to the already swirling dust and chaos.

The horses still roped together, bolted towards the open trail heading north. Kelly groped and staggered to his feet, swung round looking for Sam, but was drawn instinctively back to the rolling logs and the threat of whoever had unleashed them.

He tightened his grip on his Colt, sidestepped a crashing log and edged away from the barn towards the forge, keeping to the side of the slope, his gaze suddenly sharp and fixed, concentrated like a light on the dark shapes and shadows ahead.

Sam remained where he had fallen, his limbs too numb to move, his fear ice-cold at his spine. He blinked the sweat from his eyes and stared after the crouched, creeping silhouette of Kelly as he drew ever closer to the forge.

Had he seen something, heard something above the crash and spin of the logs? Was someone waiting there? Sam swallowed. Maybe he should make a run for it now, get clear while he was still drawing breath, join up with Doc before it was too late.

Kelly had stopped, still crouched, still watchful, as if almost within striking distance of his quarry. The last of the logs had slithered to a halt. Now the eerie half-lit silence as dawn gathered in the east settled across Firebow like a thin gauze. Nothing moved or seemed to be alive.

Droplets of sweat eased through Sam's stubble to splash in the dirt. He could hear his own breathing, short, heavy, laboured. He shifted a leg, stretched his fingers.

Kelly had moved on, two, three, hurried steps, closing on the forge like a hunting hawk. Another half-dozen steps and he would be there. To find what, wondered Sam?

'You lookin' for me, mister?'

The voice broke through the gloom in a low, flat tone and might have come from almost anywhere. Kelly spun round to peer behind him; spun again to the left, to the right; took a step forward, then into the open in the centre of the slope where he stood his ground, legs astride, Colt held high, eyes blazing.

'That you, Carew? I guess so. Been one helluva busy fella, ain't you? My brother ain't best pleased.' Kelly looked around him anxiously. 'You goin' to show yourself, or just hide away there in the shadows?'

Sam gulped, shifted again. Hell, where was Carew? When was he going to move?

'You hearin' me, Carew?' called Kelly. There was no mistaking the anxiety and uncertainty in his voice. 'Don't know about you, but I'm plannin' on pullin' out of this soulless town right now. So are we goin' to get this done with? You got the guts when we come down to it?'

The movement at the side of the black brooding bulk of the forge drew Kelly's attention immediately. If he saw the gleam of the hip-levelled Winchester barrel, he gave no indication. Maybe the dark back-lit shape of the man brandishing it, held him transfixed. Or had he seen the man's eyes, the glint in the stare that neither blinked nor lost its tight focus?

There were seconds when both men stood as if in a timeless void where memories, images, hatreds, doubts, crowded like ghosts in a haunting of hunter and hunted. Sam could only watch, his limbs numb, his senses buried somewhere between fear and fascination.

Kelly loosed two shots from the Colt, his trigger finger working instinctively but without the conviction of the calculated shot. He could only stare, sweating and bewildered, as the dark figure at the forge did not move or so much as flinch. He levelled the gun for a third shot, gritted his teeth behind a leering grin, narrowed his eyes, clenched his free hand to a tight fist and was midway through a step forward when the Winchester finally blazed.

The line of fire came fast and furious, filling Sam's head with a roar that echoed through the empty morning, dulling his mind until he had no thoughts save those of where he was, and no sight beyond the suddenly spinning body of Chad Kelly.

When at last the Winchester's blaze was silent, there seemed only the sprawled, blood-soaked mess of the dead man for the breaking light to settle on like a bird mantling its prey.

And there was nothing of the man at the forge.

CHAPTER
TWENTY-THREE

It was a full three minutes before Sam dared to make a move. He stared for some time at the body of Chad Kelly, where already the morning flies were gathering like undertakers. He thought of the blood on the gunslinger's hands, of the best part of a life given to death, robbery, rape, destruction, to end, as perhaps he always knew it would, in the dirt of a strange town at the start of just another day. And then he thought of the bar girls heading, as they had prayed, for safety. . . .

He spat as if to clear a welling sickness from his gut and came to his feet in one rapid movement. No doubting it now, he decided, Carew would be calling the shots on this day, his next and final target being Elmore Kelly, still holed up with the Murchison spoils at the saloon.

Sam looked quickly round him. Carew, as ever, had disappeared as silently, as mysteriously as he had appeared. The horses had bolted. He stepped carefully to the dead body, picked up Kelly's Colt, slid it to his belt, and shielded his eyes against the sudden eastern glare.

Nothing to be seen or heard of Doc and the townsmen approaching. Maybe they were waiting on word from him. They could not know of the shooting of Sheriff Maloney. Well, they would have to wait. There was business here not yet finished, and Sam was determined to be there when Carew finally closed the book on the Kelly gang.

Or had Elmore still one last card to play?

Sam made his way back quickly along the route he had taken to the barn in the direction of the main street, his mind already spinning with the possibilities of what he might soon be witnessing. Would Carew choose to draw Kelly to the street for the showdown, or would he stalk him, slowly, tantalizingly, tempting him first here and then there? But Kelly was nobody's fool, and especially not now with his brothers and sidekicks dead and nothing between him and the dirt worms than a drawn gun, a fast shot and a whole heap of the luck that always seemed to sit on a gunslinger's shoulders. Until, that is, the day of reckoning.

Sam hurried on, moving swiftly through the stacked timbers, past the tumbledown shack to the rear of the mercantile and then on to the door to the disused saddlery where he climbed as fast as his legs would take him to the room overlooking the street.

All quiet, not a movement save the skim of a fly. The morning gathered its full light. Sam could only watch.

*

A half-hour passed. It seemed like an hour, thought Sam, wiping the sweat from his face for the twentieth time. He felt his shirt tight in its stickiness across his back. He shifted his position at the window and scanned the street once again. Empty. Not so much as a fly. Only the shadows. But Kelly was there somewhere, damn it, and it had to be the saloon. He would never stray a step more than necessary from the money.

As for Carew . . . That man was like the light on a showery day: never around for long, always on the move, flitting and skipping about faster than a moon-dazed moth. Patience, that was his edge; patience, a deadly aim and the cold indifference to walk away when it was done. But, hell, he sure must have had some deep-seated hatred to pursue the Kellys like he had for so long. And when it was over, what then? Would he stay, explain himself, ride out, shift like the light?

A movement. A shadow across the saloon-bar window, then a shape at the batwings. There and then gone. Kelly was on the move. But he had no horse and not much hope of getting to one. Carew would have scattered any spare mounts.

Sam wiped his face again. Kelly could opt for a showdown with Carew. Call him out and stand face-to-face. Or he could take what he could comfortably carry of the money and make a run for it. But how far would he get in this heat through a bone-dry country?

Sam squinted for a sight of the shape. There it was again, emerging at the batwings, watching. He could see the glint in the eyes, the concentration in their unblinking stare.

Kelly had made up his mind. He was coming out.

The 'wings creaked like old bones in tired joints as Kelly pushed through them, let them swing closed behind him and stood to his full height, perfectly still on the boardwalk. He had belted twin Colts at his waist, their butts clean and clear of the holsters. His broad-brimmed hat was set low to give the maximum shade to his eyes which, even as Sam watched at a distance from across the street, shifted rapidly, scanning to his left, then to the right, moving higher, lowering again, staring ahead, back to the left, the right, never still. A thin beading of sweat gleamed in his stubble. His arms rested easy at his sides, his fingers flexing lightly as if caught in some soft breeze.

He took a step forward to the edge of the boardwalk. 'Know you're out there, Carew,' he called in a flat, level voice. 'Can guess what happened to Chad. He never made it, eh? Same as my brother Bonehead never did, not to mention a whole heap of my associates. Got to hand it to you, Marshal, you know your business sure enough. A fine, upstandin' man of the law. Well, let's see just how fine and upstandin'. Time's come, Carew. You all set?'

Sam swallowed nervously and licked at fresh sweat as Kelly's voice settled across the morning like one of the spreading shadows. He pressed closer to the window to glance along the deserted street. Nothing to left, nothing to right. He swallowed again and blinked rapidly.

Kelly stood firm, still as tall and straight on the boardwalk. 'Been a long whiles, Carew,' he called again. 'How many years now we been crossin' trails – three, four, mebbe more, eh? You bet. Recall them days back at Williamstown, then Princeville, Standin' Rocks, railroad out of Juniper. . . . Ain't that where I shot that deputy of yours at the time; the fella some reckoned was your son? Well, if it was, then you'll be knowin' how I feel right now at the loss of kin. T'ain't exactly a cheery feelin', is it? Nossir, not one bit. But. . . .'

His voice trailed away for a moment as if to dwell on some unspoken recollection. 'Hell,' murmured Sam to himself, 'if that don't take the real biscuit. Who'd have thought . . . Carew's son, f'Cris'sake.'

Kelly stepped from the boardwalk to a patch of shade in the street. 'Yeah, well,' he continued, his eyes alive again as his glances probed and sifted every wall, window, doorway; every yard, it seemed, of clapboard and planking, 'I got to thinkin' some while I've been waitin' on you, Carew, and it figures in my book that we should call a truce on all this. How about that? I got enough money back there in the bar to set us both up for whatever years we've still got comin'. So what say we call this off? We split the Murchison money fifty-fifty, straight down the middle, and ride out of this two-bit town free to go wherever we so choose. No messin', no double dealin', you got my word on it.'

Kelly licked his lips, then blew cooling air across the tips of his fingers. He shifted the weight of his stance, adjusted his hat against the gathering sweat and deepened his glare on the street. 'You hearin' me loud and clear, Carew?' he called. 'I hope I ain't wastin' my breath here.'

Sam swallowed and pressed closer to the window. What now, he wondered? When would Carew show himself? Where was he holed up? How long. . . ?

He saw the shadow begin to reach across the far end of the street only seconds before Kelly had it in his range of vision.

Carew came slowly but deliberately from the boardwalk to the centre of the street and turned without haste or hesitation to face Elmore Kelly.

'Well, well,' grinned Kelly, shifting his weight again, 'the famous Mr Carew shows himself at last. Ain't this just somethin'! Pity you ain't got a town audience deservin' of the occasion to greet you. But, then, public appearances were never much in your repertoire, eh, Marshal? Like to keep it private, don't you?'

Kelly sauntered to the middle of the street, the sunlight streaming full on him. 'So what's the deal, my friend, or don't we have one?' He paused a moment. 'No, I guess we don't at that. Can see by the look on your face you ain't for bargainin', makin' life comfortable for yourself some place. Well, can't say you didn't have the choice. That you surely had . . . and this along of it!'

Kelly's Colts were drawn and blazing in an

instant, the spit and roar filling the street before climbing to echoes far above the rooftops.

Carew returned fire from his own drawn guns, and for a shattering few seconds it seemed to Sam that the entire world had filled with the venomous blaze and spit of gunfire.

Kelly scuffed dirt as he stumbled forward. Carew came on like a body held in the hypnotic control of a man possessed until he stopped again directly under the window from where Sam was watching.

Kelly's Colts screamed again, this time spinning a gun from Carew's right hand. The marshal faltered, part fell as a second shot kicked dirt at his boots. His grip on the second Colt weakened then collapsed to leave both guns suddenly beyond his reach.

Kelly halted, grinned, levelled his guns. 'All that money,' he croaked, 'and every last dollar of it mine. And just enough lead here to finish you, Carew, once and for all.'

Sam hoisted the sash window with one violent tug, took Chad Kelly's Colt from his belt and threw it to Carew's feet.

Kelly hesitated, fired a loose shot at the open window, but was too late then to retaliate to the blaze from Carew's burst of firing from point-blank range.

The gunslinger groaned, dropped his guns and grabbed at his gut with both hands. He shook like something caught in a fierce gust of wind, raised his eyes to Carew one last time, but did not make another sound as the marshal's Colt blazed again to level a clean shot through his head.

Seconds later the reign of the Kelly gang was over.

CHAPTER TWENTY-FOUR

The cool rustle of the night breeze eased through the batwings of the Palace hotel, disturbing the trails of dust, shimmering through an ancient cobweb and dimming for a moment the soft flame in the newly primed and lit lantern on the saloon-bar table.

'So that's how it was, Mr Chace,' said Caleb Carr pouring two measures of whiskey from a dusty bottle. 'That's how my pa saw it with his own eyes. He was right there, 'cross the ways, on the other side of the street at the window in the one-time saddlery. Place is still standin', still there, and the window along of it. And I could show you the exact spot – exact, mind you – where Elmore Kelly fell and died that day.'

'Bet you could, too,' said Chace, fingering his glass of whiskey, 'but that ain't the complete end of the story is it, Caleb? Not quite, eh? What happened later that day? Do you know what happened?'

'Sure, I was right alongside of Doc Parker and the others when they finally rode in. I saw and heard it all, same as if it were yesterday. Pa told his story of what he had seen of the gunnin' of Chad and Elmore, but explained that by the time he had run down from the room in the saddlery Carew had gone. Just vanished, and him with a wounded hand at that. All that Pa was left with was dead bodies.'

'And then what?' asked Chace. 'Did they find Carew?'

'No, never did. Searched the town top to bottom, but there was no sign or sight of him. He'd had his horse hidden away and he just rode out. North, south, east, west . . . we don't know. Could've gone anywhere, but that was the last we saw of him.' Caleb finished his drink in one gulp. 'But Carew weren't the real priority at that point, even though he'd taken on the Kelly gang darn near single-handed. No, it was the news Doc Parker and the men broke to Pa later that mornin'. That was the first nail, as Pa put it, in Firebow's coffin.'

Chace eased back carefully in his rickety chair. 'Go on,' he murmured.

'Doc said as how the townsfolk had had a proper meetin' out at Bottom Creek after the killin' of Casey and the bar girls to discuss their future. Some reckoned as how it'd only be a matter of time to put the town back to normal once Kelly and his men had either ridden out or been eliminated. Others weren't so sure. They argued that

157

the place was stained with blood and death and no good would ever come of livin' on with the memories in the shadow of the place, and that leavin' the town and the evils it had witnessed to its own fate was the best thing to do. Abandon it, pull out, go start again some place else and make a new life, they said, if only for the sake of the young ones.'

Caleb paused a moment. 'Long and the short of it, Mr Chace, was that those for pullin' out won the day. They collected what was worth takin', loaded their wagons and pulled out headin' west that very day. All except Pa and me.'

'And why did he stay?'

'Pa reckoned as how there was still a livin' to be made off this land and he would stay and prove it. Build a home for him and me and settle it like a proper spread – which is exactly what he did, and saw it finished and me full grown before the Good Lord summoned him. Yessir, a proper home, clean and decent and a happy place. He had no regrets and neither have I.'

'So it was just you and your pa?' said Chace.

'That was the way of it. Pa said as how Doc might've stayed, but Doc figured it was his duty to stick with the townsfolk 'til they were settled again, and to return the stolen money to the bank at Murchison, specially seein' as how we had no sheriff now. Pa understood that well enough, though Doc said as how he would get back one day. He never did.'

Chace sighed. 'And Carew – what of him?'

'We never saw or had proper word of him again,

though I know that Pa secretly believed he would show up one day. Time to time when folk drifted through reg'lar enough in the early days, Pa would ask after him. Did anybody know him, know of him, or heard of him? But, no, nobody had, and soon after the visitors didn't come, and folk just didn't give a damn for Firebow. It just died. Pretty soon we were a ghost town much as you see it now. Time passed, Pa built the homestead like he said he would, and then he died. No fuss, no pain, just went to sleep one night and didn't bother with the new day. Said as how he'd go like that. Leave the start of the next day to me, he said. He figured I'd know what to do.' Caleb paused again in quiet reflection. 'Buried him out on his land there in the shade of a tree where he used to sit and smoke most nights.' He paused again. 'And the shot-through silver dollar piece he always carried after the day of the shootin'. Buried that along of him, too.'

'Dollar piece?'

'Pa always said as how he found it right next to the body of Elmore Kelly. Been shot clean through at some time. He swore that Carew had tossed it there that mornin'. Mebbe, mebbe not, but Pa always reckoned for it bein' his lucky piece. Kept it with him all the time.'

'Fascinatin',' said Chace. He finished his drink and came to his feet. 'I'm obliged to you, young man. I think I know more about Firebow now and what happened here than I figured possible. The long ride was worth it.' He smiled. 'But for now, it's

159

time to move on again.'

'Hey, there's no hurry, Mr Chace. Gettin' to be full dark out there. You're more than welcome to stay at the homestead. There's a spare room and most things necessary. Real comfort. Be glad to have you. You could see where Pa's buried.'

'That'd be good, but I reckon not. These old bones need to be movin'. I get too settled any place and I may not want to leave!' He smiled again. 'Meantime, it's been a real pleasure meetin' you, and I wish you well out there on your homestead. My bettin' would be one of these days there's goin' to be a little lady there to share it with you, and soon a family. I'd lay to that, young Caleb, definitely.'

Chace adjusted his hat and moved towards the batwings. 'Oh,' he said, turning, 'and thanks for the drink. I'll pay for it.'

'No need,' gestured Caleb. 'There's still a few bottles around the place – if you know where to look!'

'Well, I'll leave this for old-time's sake then.' Chace delved in his waistcoat pocket and laid a coin on the table. 'Pass it on to your son some day.' He nodded, walked to the 'wings and, without looking back or another word, disappeared into the night.

Caleb Carr watched the man go, then picked up the coin and held it against the flickering light of the lantern.

A silver dollar piece, shot clean through.

H

Pwc